STRANGE ECHOES

Bleeding Edge Books
www.bleedingedgepub.com

STRANGE ECHOES

EDITED BY

D. ALEXANDER WARD
& GINA SCAPELLATO

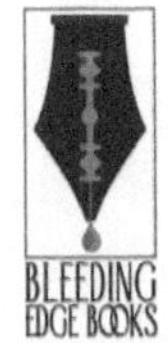

BLEEDING
EDGE BOOKS

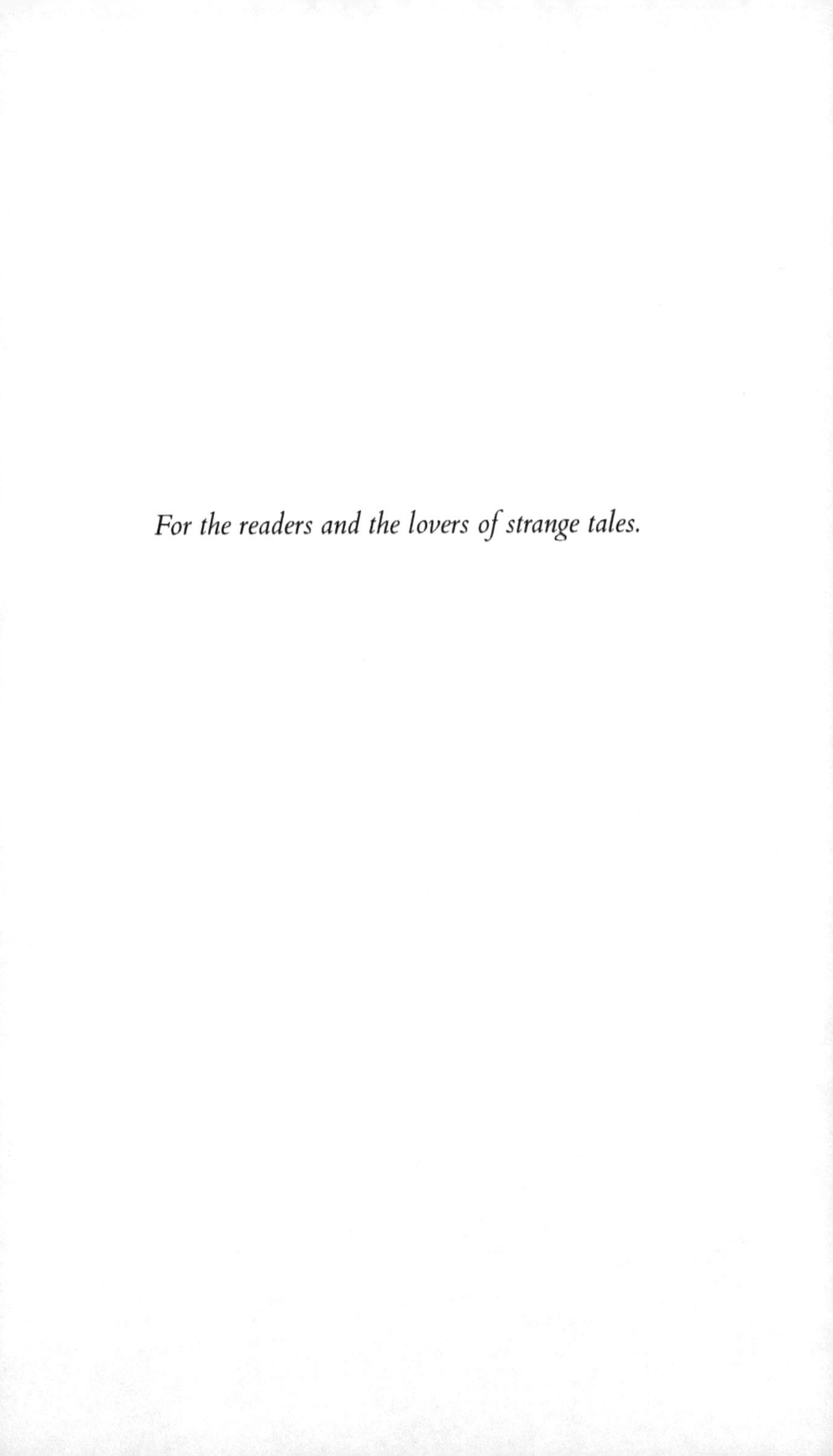

For the readers and the lovers of strange tales.

Table of Contents

Canyon Country

by Pamela M. Durgin

The wind scoured her face as she walked along the shoulder. It carried sand and bits of sage, ripped from the tumbleweeds climbing up barbed wire fencing on either side of the road. She kept her head down to keep the road dust out of her eyes. A gritty film already plastered the skin on her face, arms, and legs. Sweat dried almost instantly in the hot Santa Ana *devil winds* but not before a layer of grime attached itself.

The heat made her head pound, or maybe it was the remnants of alcohol still poisoning her. She focused on her feet, the scraped toes of her boots and the asphalt sliding under them. She knew where she was going, the strip mall, but she wasn't sure exactly how far it was.

She had been babysitting. She walked out, no one to stop her. The squalling ricocheting in her skull, then the sudden silence. More of a presence than the screaming wad of flesh had been. They wouldn't be home for another few hours. Then they would find the mess and start the search. Hysteria and recriminations. Her parents would be questioned.

She was impulsive, sometimes savagely impulsive. That's what her dad said.

"What the fuck were you thinking?!" he would bellow before grounding her for some transgression that was surely a sign of worse to come. Mostly, he was right. The confrontations occurring over and over, her dad sometimes overcome by the rage that comes from seeing yourself in your offspring, a monster. The last time calling her a slut, stupid, vicious, before her mom grabbed his wrist, as he reached for her neck. Shaking her off, he stomped out to the garage and slammed the door. His words meant nothing, but her mother's wounded eyes caused a flicker, but only a flicker, of sadness.

———————————

Alice wandered along the two-lane road in Canyon Country. Bleak, sun bleached hills lined either side of the road, with dirt bike and 4x4 tracks scarring the steep inclines. Occasional rocky outcroppings competed with sage and other chaparral, low to the ground, breaking up the brown and red of the dirt. A Martian landscape, inhospitable, desolate. They used to film westerns in these hills and sometimes she'd come across old structures that looked like film sets. But mostly it was just dirt, rocks, and tumbleweeds.

The strip mall was some distance ahead. She would wait at the 7-Eleven. Although they bored her, Troy or Steve would make for a brief distraction. They had cars and cruised the strip malls, weary just like her, looking for something to do. Or, maybe someone else, someone new, would cross her path.

Her backpack was uncomfortably heavy, sodden, digging into her shoulders, the weight at the bottom yielding, still warm. Sweat and fluids slimy against her back. There would be a smell soon.

Shielding her eyes with one hand, she looked up the road and saw the sign, still small in the distance, shimmering in the heat. The sun directly overhead, she thought if she touched the top of her scalp, she would burn herself. No cars passed, nothing moved except the tumble weeds pushed by the dry, hot wind. As she got closer, she could see the vague shape of a burnt orange El Camino nosed up to the back door of the 7-Eleven. The glass of the other store fronts winked in the sun, blurring together in a tan mass. The green and red of the convenience store the only color. It looked like a couple of other cars were in front of the far end of the strip. Probably at the laundromat. The sun-blasted parking lot could have been the surface of the moon, it was so distant and alien. The heat was oppressive. She felt in the pockets of her cut-offs. The folded bills and loose change were still there.

She crossed the parking lot and eyed the metal igloo ice cooler hunched on the sidewalk. She thought about how good it would feel to crawl inside, close the metal door, and go to sleep. She pushed into the store and as the bell went off above her head, the clerk, owner of the El Camino, looked up from his car magazine. An angry smear of acne swept across his forehead and his rat-like face was framed by a tangle of greasy blond hair that hung to his shoulders. He swept his eyes over her and, instantly losing interest, looked back down at the car mag. She browsed the Hostess rack while she gauged whether he would sell her beer. No, she would have to wait outside for someone to ask. She thought about a Schlitz Malt Liquor tall and how that would take the edge off. She'd have to settle for the Slurpee for now.

Approaching the counter, she fished a bill out of her pocket and slid it in front of the magazine.

"Large Cherry Coke Slurpee."

He grunted. Without looking at her, he took the money, rang up the sale, gave her the change, then turned to the machine. She had never seen anything move so slow. Well, maybe a sloth. She had giggled at the footage of a poor sloth slowly, slowly climbing along a branch on a National Geographic show, or was it Mutual of Omaha's Wild Kingdom? She stifled a laugh as she watched him pull the lever of the Slurpee machine. His t-shirt stuck to his back. The air conditioning wasn't working. The inside of the store was just as hot as the parking lot. She gratefully grabbed the cold cup from his hand and pressed it to her forehead before walking outside.

She sat on the curb at the side of the store, next to the ice machine. The machine chugged and cycled. The only other sound was the lazy churring of grasshoppers in the dried knee-high grass that bent and swirled in anemic patches out beyond the asphalt. She surveyed the lot and surroundings from her perch in the shade.

"Earthquake weather", she muttered as the hot, dry wind lifted her hair and sent a crumpled Marlboro cigarette pack skittering past her toes.

The icy slush cooled her and she stretched her bare legs out before her, leaning back on the pack. The gravel scattered across the concrete curb bit into the backs of her legs, but she didn't move. The heat trapped in the cement dried her sweat, crusting her with salt. She put the cup between her thighs, the icy condensation providing instant relief.

The rumble of an engine from the opposite end of the lot caught her attention and she turned to see a battered white truck, a work truck with toolboxes, pull into a spot in front of the store. The sun reflected off the dusty windshield, obscuring the cab. Work boots, faded jeans, and black t-shirt. Stocky with a shock of black hair. She waited to see if he noticed her. He only looked ahead.

"Excuse me."

He stopped and looked over, at first only seeming to see the ice machine. She stood, brushing the gravel from her butt purposely. He saw her then and a smile crawled across his face without reaching his eyes. Dead eyes, flat black, square jaw, and white teeth. Something thrummed inside her.

"I was wondering… umm… I left my ID at home and…"

"You want me to buy you booze…"

Laughing, "Well yeah, I mean, if you don't mind…"

"You know that's illegal. I could get in trouble."

"It's not like I'm underage. I just lost my ID…"

"I thought you said you left it at home."

"Yeah, that's what I meant." Her faced burned.

She no longer cared if he agreed to buy the beer; she was eager to keep his attention. He had a gravelly voice somehow older than his face. He looked mid to late 20s, but weary. His eyes though… she had to focus on other things… his nose, mouth, a spot to the side of his head. His eyes held no humanity. Something about him sent a shiver through her, not an unpleasant sensation. She thought of pulling the tail of a tiger, hoping for a hungry gaze to be turned upon her. She suspected he would disappoint her like so many others had.

"Since I'm taking such a chance here, I'll only do this if you agree to share a beer with me." His eyes now locked on hers.

"Okay," she whispered.

He nodded and turned to go in without asking for money or what she wanted. She watched him stride into the store; muscles shifted under his damp t-shirt.

For just a moment, jagged anticipation of what comes next, pleasure, or pain, flooded her with endorphins. Like an addict, she thrummed with possibility. Her restlessness is for this, this feeling right now. Other things don't work like this except… then pushed it out of her mind. It seemed like mere seconds had passed when he appeared at the driver's side of his truck with a bag.

"Well, are you coming?"

She stepped, a little too quickly, to the passenger door. She had to try pushing the button a couple times before it opened. He was leaning across the bench seat, having opened it from the inside.

"It sticks…"

She climbed in a little self-consciously, feeling her cut offs riding up between her legs, she tugged on the outside of her shorts to reposition them as she hoisted her backpack onto the floor between her feet. He didn't seem to notice. She was disappointed.

A rosary swung from the rearview mirror, tracing small arcs in the center of the windshield as it was pushed by a hot gust of wind. Cheap metal links, green with oxidation, linked red glass beads and a blackened crucifix. It was wrapped so tightly around the rearview mirror as to give the impression of strangulation. The brown paper bag crackled like fire next to her. She looked in the bag. Tops of a six pack of something and a pint bottle.

She presented a smile, purposeful, ready, and said, "Where are we going?"

Not looking at her, "A place I'm staying right now. It's a ranch. You'll like it." And then, "Do you like horses?"

"I love horses!" Surprising herself. Realizing that the fifteen-year-old she was had just shown herself.

The sun was magnified through the windshield and she thought her thighs would burst into flames. The windows were down, but the air felt like a blast furnace. He whistled under his breath, tunelessly. She thought for a moment, *This is a bad idea.* Instead of dwelling on that, she said, "What's your name?"

He laughed. It was the same sound her dog made when he choked on a bone. She tensed and waited.

"Call me Joe."

Before she could stop herself, she blurted, "That's my dog's name."

"Well then, you won't forget it." Without affectation, flat. His smile still in place. He didn't ask her name and she didn't offer it.

She didn't see another car. She knew the main road well, but as he made a series of turns onto smaller county roads further into the brown hills, she lost track of where she was. She had never been this far into Canyon Country. She thought, with a twinge of regret or maybe dull anger, that her dad would like it out here. He liked to take his 4x4 up into the hills and crawl up the dirt gullies of the parched landscape. He would take Joe, always, and sometimes her and her mom. It was his 'thinking time' so they weren't usually welcome.

In the clatter and rumble of road noise and the hot air, she felt like she was suffocating. Something – anticipation or maybe self-preservation – signaled her, causing a burning in her stomach. She didn't listen, she never listened.

Examining his profile, she willed him to look at her. Wanting to get the game going. He stared straight ahead. He was still smiling, or maybe he was gritting his teeth, the sound of his whistling a sinister undercurrent. His profile was alarmingly handsome, but his manner and his eyes were cold, distant.

She swallowed. Her mouth was so dry she choked and started to cough. He reacted by slapping her on the back, "You aren't going to die on me, are you?" Issuing another bark, her eyes teared from choking.

"Here it is."

The truck turned between two rotted posts. One had a NO TRESSPASSING sign nailed to it. The words were almost obscured by bullet holes. Rusted barbed wire writhed between gray posts stuck in the dried dirt. The winds had stacked dried sagebrush tumbleweeds intermittently along the fence line. It continued out of sight into a ravine and reappeared to climb the adjacent hill. She thought the chaparral and tumbleweeds somehow softened the sharp, dangerous angles of the fence as it sought out the soft places to cut through. She shook her head, dislodging the thought. A structure loomed far up the dirt road. She couldn't make out the rest of the compound, but it appeared to have a few vehicles already parked around it. As the truck bounced up the road, a rooster tail of red dust obscured that rear view.

I won't be coming back this way again.

There was a surprising amount of vegetation, but it was all brown and dry. It smelled like baking dust and something dead. A skinny, mange-ridden horse stood with one hoof held up off the ground as if injured.

"See, there's a horse!" He pointed. Still not looking at her.

As they approached the house, she saw a faded blue Ford truck with a dented camper parked to the side, a brick red Volkswagen bug with a broken back window, a faded gold K-car, and as they pulled up to the front, she saw the back end of a trailer on cinder blocks parked in the back.

Getting out of the truck, Joe grabbed the bag from the floorboard. He slammed the door and walked to the front of the truck. Seeing that she was not moving, he looked at her for the first time since they left the 7-Eleven.

"You promised!" He held up the bag.

She didn't move. Joe slowly walked to her door and pulled. It opened on the first try for him, the squeal of hinges making her flinch. He stood holding the door, the paper bag under his arm, and stared at her. It was like looking at a mannequin. His expression was bland. A smile curled his lips, but his eyes were flat. She unstuck her legs from the upholstery, imagining that she was leaving strips of flesh on the vinyl.

She could hear voices and laughter and dogs barking, but there was no sign of who was making the sounds. *They're in the house*, she thought. Standing next to the truck looking up into Joe's dead face, she involuntarily touched her head as if to see if it were still attached. Her hair was damp with sweat and gritty with road dirt, her skin crusted with salt.

"Can I have a beer?"

Wordlessly he reached into the sack and produced a tall can of Schlitz Malt Liquor. As she opened it and looked at the condensation rolling down the silver bull, she wondered how he knew that she drank this crap. He watched her chug half the can and nodded his approval. The cool of the beer was replaced by the comforting heat of the alcohol settling into her. Momentarily fortified, she started towards the house.

He grabbed her arm and said "No, no, we're going back here." Nodding towards the trailer, he led her around to the back of the building.

The trailer was parked at an angle behind the main house. The knee-high grass underneath and around the trailer had dried to straw, creating a nest at the end of the dirt area encircling the house and parking area in front. No one had bothered to cut it back for a long time and she thought for a moment, *this is a fire hazard*, having watched many grass fires in these hills from her bedroom window. The wind gusts reminding her of her blow dryer and again she thought of 'earthquake weather,' the strange catch-all for the warm, windy, sometimes overcast, weather that seems to bring catastrophe.

Joe led the way along a path through the grass to the warped wooden steps at the trailer door. They had moved away from the house, and she could now see the back. Aluminum windows were covered with stained sheets except one where the jagged edges of broken glass were evident. Someone had wedged a piece of cardboard into the window frame to cover the hole. Pastel blue, green and yellow stripes splotched with brown in one window and giant daisies rendered obscene with yellowish stains hung in another. She noticed a pipe jutting from the back of the house, a blackish slime drooling from it into an open cesspool below. Flies rose in waves as the wind dislodged them from something, a small animal, a foot or so away from the hole. The smell swept over her in a gust, the heat and the odor curdling her insides. She stumbled. He caught her, his grip tighter than necessary.

Cackling rose in a wave like the flies from the back of the house. *Is someone watching us?* She thought. She strained to see if she could glimpse a face through the threadbare sheets, but they only bulged and sucked through the open windows with the wind gusts. No person appeared.

"Is someone else here?"

"Nope. Just us."

"I heard voices, laughing…and the cars." He stopped and turned, dramatically cupping his ear to listen, "I only hear the wind…" His pantomime was more denigrating than clownish. *You're crazy*, it said.

Impatiently, he kicked open the door and pulled her inside. The heat was worse inside than out. The windows were open, and the smell of the cesspool swirled in the hot air. She glanced around. A colonial hunting party marched along wallpaper that was in surprisingly good condition and her footsteps crunched on stiff olive-green shag carpeting that wasn't. Piles of clothes littered the floor, a small TV perched on a metal stand, and a sink overflowed with dirty dishes. No severed heads, no dead bodies. Alice slumped. The feeling of danger ebbed as she looked around the sordid space.

Alice dropped her sodden backpack onto the floor, pushed dirty clothes off a sagging couch, and flopped onto a concave cushion with an exaggerated bounce that only served to bruise her tail bone. The fabric was a rough weave of faded orange, yellow, and brown plaid. She imagined fleas, mites, and ticks nestled in the stuffing.

"Nice place you got here."

She hoped the sarcasm in her voice would trigger a reaction, but he just drained his beer and stared at her, his eyes flat. He unbuckled his belt and she started to laugh, probing for a sore spot, an insecurity, hoping to get the game going. Instead, he stepped toward her and, looping his fingers into the waist of her shorts, pulled her up to him.

Twenty minutes of shoving, grasping, fingers digging at soft parts, his hot tongue sloppy in her mouth and on her face. Sour sweat, grunting, the mild violence of it the only stimulation for her. No moments on the edge, wondering if it would go too far. The disappointment of it settled on her, a mute companion that clung to her only lifting briefly, like the moment she silenced the crying…

Sweat still damp in her hair, her thighs, and buttocks sticky with his cum, he grasped her hand and pulled her to the floor. On their knees, naked facing each other, grit embedded in the shag carpeting biting into her, she watched his face. His eyes were closed, dark lashes damp from sweat, or maybe tears; he held both her hands and began to pray. She had a flicker of interest, hoping for hellfire and damnation.

The trailer was dark except for the shafts of light cutting through the ripped curtains. Dust motes swirled, circling an invisible drain. Alice watched his face as he prayed fervently.

"Forgive me my weakness. Show me discipline, spare not the barbs. The whore temptress kneels before you, ready, as am I, for your wrath. We are ready for the cleansing flames."

"Give me a fucking break!" Pulling her hands away, she got to her feet. "You're pathetic."

He looked at her, no sign of recognition in his eyes. Then slowly he seemed to return, blinking and rubbing his face as he stood and started to dress. Not a ripple of anger or even interest.

It was so fucking hot. The Santa Ana, *Mal*, winds pushed their way into the trailer, carrying the smell of smoke and stirring the lazy flies from the mess in the sink. Buzzing mixed with a dog barking outside.

She stumbled to the kitchenette and wiped her crotch with a sour dish rag, tossing it back onto the counter. Looking into the sink clotted with food remnants, she saw a steak knife.

He watched, silently, as she dressed. His face was slack; gone was the smart-ass and the repentant sinner. A benign tumor on the earth. She hated him for not even striving for malignancy. He walked out to the truck and waited for her.

She picked up her backpack, reached into the sink for the knife, slipping it into her back pocket. She slammed the trailer door open and stepped onto the cracked earth, crushing the dried brush, and walked past the truck. When he yelled after her, she said she would walk back. He protested. The most animated he had been except when he came.

"It's probably ten miles. You can't walk."

Turning back to him, she stood looking at his sweating face. She walked to the open driver's side window and stepped up on to the running board. His face expectant, awaiting a kiss, perhaps.

"I forgive you," she said.

She pulled the rusty steak knife from her pocket and, with her left hand, plunged it into the left side of his neck just under his ear. He stiffened, eyes wide, as she drew the knife across his throat. Bloody bubbles formed under that strong jaw, his eyes grateful.

She watched him for a moment and waited for a feeling, a sensation, but felt nothing. She turned and walked to the house listening to the strange wet sounds, gurgling like the fish tank she had as a kid. She glanced back at his wide eyes, pink bubbles under his chin, a sheet of red coloring the flesh of his neck, darkening the front of his t-shirt. The wind carried smoke and a hot, fetid smell.

———•———

As she approached the house, the stench was eye watering. She couldn't tell if she was headed toward the smell or carrying it. Laughter and voices floated from the open windows. She heard the dog barking again. The old horse whinnied asthmatically from the front of the house.

On the tips of her toes, she pulled herself up into the window. Pushing through the stained daisy sheet, she sat on the sill and then dropped into the room. The floors were soft with rot. The room was sparsely furnished: a bedframe, a chair. Wallpaper hung in strips from the walls, a floral print, and the ceiling was puckered and peeling from years of roof leaks. Rodent droppings were everywhere. She crept into the hall, now silent. Standing still in the empty hallway, she waited for the voices. Nothing but the wind and the rustle and thump in Joe's truck as he, in his death throes, abandoned her. He was already dead inside, like she was. She turned back to her new distraction.

She was sure she would turn the corner and find a house full of people and barking dogs. She continued her search. She moved from room to room, finding nothing but rotting timber, cracked porcelain, rotting animal carcasses: some birds, a cat, possibly a coyote. She stopped at a back room - a room from which she was sure she heard crying. Stained circus-themed wallpaper still clung to the walls. Stained, bulging seals balanced balls on the tips of their noses while strangely skinny clowns capered and grinned, holding tiny parasols. The floor was littered with broken glass, feathers, and animal feces. She leaned against the wall and as the alcohol, heat and exhaustion overwhelmed her, she slid down the wall and sat, legs stretched out in front of her, like she had done at the 7-Eleven. The grit and dried rat shit ground into the backs of her legs, her palms. She closed her eyes. Wind buffeted the house, creaks and groans moved with intention through the rooms, carrying soft voices, laughing. She didn't move or open her eyes. She surrendered. A wheezing cackle, a crying infant, voices soft, then raised in anger; a dog panting and whimpering. All moving from room to room, seeking escape.

•———————•

She was thrust into sound and light. The smoke stung her throat and eyes. As she surfaced from sleep, she heard the old horse whinny again, this time in panic, and the sound of uneven galloping receded into the distance as a dull roar swelled and brought her fully awake. She felt her face. It was wet. She thought she must have been crying in her sleep. She tried to breathe in but coughed instead. Then the sound of the wind, and something else, a sustained scream, like a wild animal.

She rubbed her eyes and as they adjusted, she could see it was night, but everything glowed. Flickering shadows played across black eyed seals and clowns. Smoke hung in the room. A glow flickered through the edges of the broken window glass. The cardboard in the window curled and began to smoke. It fell away to reveal a swirl of orange embers dancing in the night sky. Up behind the house on the hill, a molten line of flame rolled fluidly over dried grass, climbing over the trailer, then the truck and Joe, withering in the cab. The flames looked sentient, reaching, grasping then hopping like hellish fairies sprinkling embers. It was beautiful. The heat began to blister her skin. She strained to keep her burning eyes open.

Was this the cleansing conflagration Joe had prayed for?

The movement within the fire line was coalescing; figures emerged. Dogs and coyotes, jumping, yipping, and howling, though she couldn't hear them, only see their muzzles stretching and curling. A large feline crept along low to the ground, stalking the canines, its fur bubbling and rippling like lava. Ravens, hawks, chickens, rising on glowing wings, sizzling, and swooping. A figure, maybe a woman, running towards her before folding in on herself; trying, it seemed, to duck behind something she thought would save her. The higher pitch of a scream reached her, sharp as a whistle. Faces surfaced, pressed out from the wall of flame. Small figures, children huddled together. She thought of a scout troop..

Her breath came in scalding gulps, the anticipation of burning alive causing her to tremble. A buzzing like an electrical charge climbed up her spine and shot through her limbs. She felt the vibration and contraction in her abdomen and the pleasure-pain of the pulse caused her to gasp. Thinking of the weight in her backpack, the weight she had carried inside her for nine months. She relived the moment she stopped its screaming, stopped its squirming. She had the same feeling, the pulse. The aftermath, though, was numbness, workman-like dismantling then bundling of the small corpse, as if to fix what was broken. But she knew nothing could fix this, nothing could undo what was done, and nothing could contain what was released inside her. Her mind revisited, savored the feeling several times while she walked the blasted landscape of Canyon Country.

She watched the wall of flames approaching, bringing all it had consumed. She stretched, reached out, welcoming the conflagration into her bosom.

She could hear the restless shuffling of the others. Crying, laughing, whimpering, coughing, barking, whining, bleating. So many waiting for release. She didn't turn as she pulled her backpack, its contents now quivering, to the front of her. Bracing herself, the pack pressed into her abdomen, she felt them against the back of her body. Skin, fur, tongues, wet noses, sticky hands large and small. She leaned into the window frame and smiled as orange, white and yellow embers showered onto the grass around the trailer. They looked like fireworks or stars sweeping across the dark sky, bringing with them the blistering, cleansing heat on Santa Ana winds.

A black swirling mass encircled the structure,

dragging the liquid fire in its wake. Something, the trailer or truck, exploded and jagged pieces of sheet metal hurtled through the window on a fireball as she smiled, cradling her backpack and the small shape within.

Author's Note on "Canyon Country"

This story was inspired by my wanderings as a teenage runaway in Southern California. I spent many hours hitch-hiking, hanging out, getting in trouble. The neat and orderly suburbs where I grew up were surrounded by old movie ranches, carrot fields, and fire-scarred canyons. I am very interested in bleak, open landscapes and exploring those spaces and probing how those landscapes can influence the people who move through them.

About the Author

PAMELA DURGIN is a writer from San Francisco where she lives with her husband and three cats. This is her first published story.

Links
Facebook: facebook.com/pameladurgin

Hitching a Sacrificial Anode to a Well-Appointed Metal Monstrosity

by Starlene Justice

I've been called paranoid, but I prefer to think of myself as a careful kind of guy—maybe just observant to a fault. Take my observations of lizards, for example. I can tell you that they have very specific territories. In a yard that's about a quarter of an acre, there could conceivably be somewhere between 50 to 70 lizards living on that property. But they don't just run around willy-nilly. There might be a certain group that lives in the sandy area near the back doorstep and another group that darts around on the other side of the house in the trees and shrubs. Yet another batch stakes out their territory in the front yard. There are probably three to four different species and they will be a mix of male and female. All these years of living in the same house, I've come to be able to tell the difference.

For some of the species, there may be only five or fewer individuals. For other species, 50 or more. Careful observation will allow a person to come to recognize many, many different individuals. Their habits and their territory will be familiar.

I am not a scientist. I am not even a herpetologist—though it seems as if anyone who knows that word *should* be one. I am just a regular guy. Or, at least, I like to think so. Just observant, like I said.

Up here in the village, where most of the streets slope drastically to sea level, I try to find unique routes for my daily walks so that I don't have to strain myself too much. I'm not lazy, just strategic. On these walks, it's possible to observe a lot of things.

The population here seems to be equally divided between the real and the surreal. Run-of-the mill families with kids, then thieves and drug addicts. Seaside communities can be a lot like mountain communities: you get the rich, and you get the crazy. Well, I'm being nice. I didn't mention the pervs and sociopaths.

The house I'm standing in front of and looking

at right now always gives me the feeling that the resident—who is the owner and *only* employee at the feed store a few miles south of here—has a wife no one knows about that he keeps locked up in his basement. This guy's radar is just way-too-acutely focused on the criminal and law-enforcement activity around here. Like he's got a stake in keeping tabs. Every time I stop by to pick up some rabbit food, he goes on and on about the dope-heads—like they're the one and only problem in society. Freaks me out.

Pretty sure he's a closet homosexual, too. Whenever I hand him money to pay for my five pounds of alfalfa pellets and sack of timothy hay, I swear he makes a point to touch my hand when he returns the change. I don't mind if he *is* homosexual, and that's the truth of it. I just think it's weird to be covert about it.

Is there a way to tell someone's sexual orientation by looking at their house? I bet there is. That's what I'm wondering right now, but this house is just plain old nondescript. White wood paneling, old stone fireplace, white drapes on clean windows. That's notable; the clean windows. I also wonder if there's a way of telling whether a house has a basement just by looking at the outside.

Next door, there's a house that's probably worth upwards of a million bucks. State-of-the-art front gate and weeds running rampant all over the yard. Plenty of territory for those lizards I mentioned. Place looks abandoned, but that gate is solid, and that house cost a mint. You can't tell me they're not growing plants on the top floor and using dark shades to block out LED lights.

I'm not going to stand here gaping too long, though. Something downright funny about a lone male standing in the street gazing at houses.

Sure enough, there's a cop car slow-trolling in the streets one block over. I can see the flash of black and white if I bend my gaze on the spaces between houses. Think I'll take this opportunity to make my way down toward the water. Haven't done that in a while. I hate the idea of the uphill climb home, but these streets are getting boring anyway. A bunch of quaint little houses painted white, or yellow, or blue-gray.. Tourists come here in droves like they've never seen the likes of such a town before. Me, I need to observe some new things. My head's getting into a fog.

I consider running down the sloping streets like a little kid, but manage to hold myself respectfully in check. After all, dogs always notice when I give in and run; they charge right into their fences and bark their fool heads off. Scares the bejeezus out of me every time.

I'm still seeing that cop car though, so I take a detour and wind my way along narrow streets out past the edges of the village. It's not a bad place to live, this town, even if I might have given a different impression earlier. Forested hills and a lively mix of old and new buildings. Nice looking church—if you go for that sort of thing. Used to be a logging town or some such, a long time ago. Mostly oil, fishing, and tourists these days. This crazy town even has some ordinance that doesn't allow planes or helicopters to fly over too low unless it's a rescue. It ruins the ambience, they say.

I'm at sea level now and I can smell the ocean and see the marshes that huddle up against the tamer, enclosed bays. No weirdos hanging about, and that's a little bit boring, too, but I can see where the ocean has pulled back and left an undrowned pathway around a rocky escarpment. I can't see past it, and the not-knowing is just killing me, so I head out that way and hope the tide doesn't rise before I can make it back in. I'm a poor swimmer, and don't much care for boats, either.

I'm curious about this sound I'm hearing. It has been slowly working its way into my consciousness like the sound of a mouse chewing a board somewhere in the attic. Only this is an industrial sound, metal gearing and the scraping of metal on metal, and metal on rock. I slow my pace and tell myself it's got to be a pumpjack—one of those rocking-horse-looking things used in offshore oil wells. We've got those all over the place here. When I see what's making the sound, I have a moment of even thinking I'm right.

The sun glints off the back of an unbelievable creature—bigger than a pumpjack, but just as metallic—glistening across a bone-like surface as black as obsidian. All bones and crooked angles with a long neck attached to an egg-shaped head. Oval eyes that seem, at first, to just be holes; but no, they are eyes. Bony ridges along its back and a concave belly (or, at least the *structure* of a belly; everything is hollow), pipes with soldered metal clumps like a platter of spareribs. Legs as tall as buildings, weirdly jointed in asymmetrical places.

At first I'm thinking someone's got a big metal sculpture out here—and how cool is that?—but when the thing starts walking across the lagoon, swaying its long neck sadly like an elephant's trunk and moaning, well then I realize things are a bit different.

It seems to be able to carry its neck either raised like a crane or level with its body. Like a diplodocus, I suppose. Don't ask me how I just retrieved that name from the dusty storage files of my brain, but there you have it. The point being: this was nothing ordinary like a giraffe. And anyway, it was *way* bigger, and what would a giraffe be doing standing in a lagoon in a sparsely populated seaside village on the coast of central California?

Right now though, its neck is lowered a bit—hang-dog style—and even though this sucker is massive, I'm not afraid of it. It has a *sad* aspect to it, which doesn't lend itself to instigating a fear reaction. In fact, I'm a little worried about it.

It comes toward me making a hollow moaning sound that perfectly mimics wind in trees, and I notice that its spiny back has something that looks like a saddle tree in the makeup of those spines, and long gear-like things near its shoulders. Just picture the levers of a tractor and you'll know what I'm talking about. Maybe this is some sort of *riding* animal.

What does me in though, is the look in this creature's eyes when it gets close enough for me to see it. Sadness, maybe. Perhaps pain. A plea for help? Rounded, glassy, and just a little bit moist. They are the only parts of the structure that do not look metallic or bony. They may be something like volcanic glass, though, now that I think about it.

The water sloshes around it as it lifts each platter-sized foot (hoof?) and sets it back down again in what looks like a strained procession of giant legs. There is a creaking sound accompanying this movement, and sometimes a grinding sound as well, and I swear this latter is making the creature wince every time it happens.

When it gets close to me, it stops and lowers its head in my direction, like a horse looking for a carrot. I ignore that heavy head for a minute and take a closer look at the metal, jointed legs. Yup, there's something wrong here, for sure. When this thing moves a certain way, I can see the joints start to gap around jagged, holey edges. It's almost like looking at a half-torn-off limb and the sight turns my stomach a bit. I can see that the creature's maker didn't account for the fact that different types of metal used together in the presence of seawater creates a battery. Now, what we've got here is the attendant corrosion. So, the poor thing's in pain, I guess.

What's needed, quite frankly, is a sacrificial anode. Why hadn't this been thought of? Now I'm irritated. Any bonehead knows that if you're going to put metal parts in wet places, you'd better have a plan for the corrosive effect. It's a pretty simple fix, too. Just add a zinc or aluminum "collar" where those other metals are coming together and the collar gets corroded before the important stuff does. I mean, catch it in time, and you never have to worry about the joints corroding; just replace the sacrificial anode. Wish it was that easy to protect my own aging joints.

By now, I'm already hatching a plan in my head for how I'm going to do this. I think zinc would work best, but it might come down to what's available.

Without really thinking about it, I splash into the shallow water where this thing is standing, reach up and give it a pat on its bony head, and then get in close to its legs. I run my hand down the part of one of its front legs that I can probably compare to the shin of a person or the cannon bone of a horse and, at the same time, make a sort of kissing noise. Sure enough, that thing picks its leg right up, like it's been schooled by a blacksmith to cooperate for shoeing.

I have to apologize to it while I look those legs over. It keeps groaning like a dinosaur—or how I think a dinosaur might groan—and I know it's not comfortable.

When I'm done, that thing just drops its head down

next to me and looks at me with those shiny, black eyes and I feel an unfortunate affection climbing into my throat. This is what I get for letting my curiosity win out. A little less observing and a little more paranoia would have served me well in this instance. Nothing for it now.

I'm a little worried that my exit from the lagoon will be regarded by this creature as abandonment, but I've got to find a fix.

"Hey!"

The voice is loud and bellowing, and I turn so fast I almost lose my balance and drop into the water.

"Get away from her!"

Her?

I look back at the creature with its haphazard metallic structure and sad eyes. That's a *female?* Well, it just goes to show you never can tell.

The man hollering at me is dressed in blue jeans and a long-sleeved shirt tucked in behind a shiny silver belt buckle. It's the belt buckle I recognize first because I know it as belonging to the man who owns the feed store and who, by the by, is the man I'm looking at.

My brain is doing a quick re-shuffle of information. No wife in the basement, probably; just a metallic creature hidden in a lagoon.

"Hurry!" he's bawling at me, and I believe that admonition is having the exact opposite effect. I feel like my legs are stuck in quicksand. "It's filling up!"

I realize, now, that this guy is in a boat, and that

the pathway I had come through on has already disappeared, and I'm probably going to have to hitch a ride with this fellow—assuming he's not prone to murdering me or something.

The man seems to be gesturing for me to get in his boat and I start to wonder about his sexual orientation again, then I decide that I really don't care at all and by now I'd find it weirder if he were straight. Such is the power of the imagination and having plenty of free time to speculate on things we can't actually know.

"She's dying," he tells me, as he lends me a hand getting into his little watercraft.

"No, no," I tell him, with conviction. "It's an easy fix. Just a sacrificial anode; that's all she needs."

"She had some," he says, revving the boat's little engine and gripping the rudder. "Aluminum. They should have been zinc. That's my fault. Just leave her be."

For some reason, I don't think to ask him what the hell she is or how the hell he made her. I don't even think to notice how we make it out of the lagoon, only that we're out of it and I can't tell how he got in. My powers of observation have come to a complete halt in the presence of so many other thoughts rattling around in my head. The only question that comes to my mind is completely absurd.

"What's her name?" I ask.

"Tessa."

I nod. As if that's a perfectly reasonable name and this is a perfectly reasonable conversation.

"You just leave her be," he reiterates.

He drops me off at the closest dock and doesn't say

a word more. I start walking—not toward my home, though—and I'm thinking how strange it is to have someone tell you to do something and then not feel at all alarmed with yourself that you know you have no intention of cooperating.

●━━━━━━━━━●

It's easy to find the materials I need. A place with boats and oil rigs needs aluminum and zinc in the way a place with horses needs stores full of hay. The harder thing will be getting these things out to the lagoon and onto the beast herself.

I do allow myself a moment to contemplate the impossibility of this creature. No heart, no lungs, no nervous system as far as I can tell. I mean, I can see through her entire structure, for God's sake. She's… empty. Yet she seems to be alive, and aware, and reactive. And female. Well, she didn't *seem* to be female, but I guess that's what she is.

Me, I'm no expert on females. Or on people, in general. I try to avoid them, most of the time. They don't get me, and I don't get them. I'm pretty sure I'm "on the spectrum," though I've never been diagnosed. Nothing wrong with a man knowing what he is and just accepting the kind of life that means for him.

I go down the next day, hoping I can remember how to get to the lagoon and, of course, I do—no problem. Considering the tides, I pick the same time of day and hope for favorable circumstances.

Tessa sees me and lifts her head from what appears

to be a slow browse of aquatic vegetation. She makes a sound that I'd be hard-pressed to describe as anything other than a snort, and then she galumphs awkwardly in my direction, moving at a rate of speed that has me suddenly worried that she might not know she should avoid running me down.

She makes such a racket with her splashing that I am compelled to glance around quickly and make sure no one is peeking around the rocks to see what all the ruckus is about. In reality, there probably isn't a living soul within a two-mile radius of this place.

I've brought a few odds and ends with me, hoping to make this endeavor a success. Wading boots, the zinc collars, of course, a flashlight, some climbing rope and grappling hooks. No idea what I'll need. It's not like Tessa has footholds built into her structure for ease of access.

Or does she?

I take a close look as I'm contemplating how to get high enough on her structure to access each of her leg joints and I notice that, while she doesn't *exactly* have clearly designated steps along her structure, there *are* some random nodules here and there, and even the occasional ledge. Yes, *ledge*. Even a system of scaffolds attached to one side of her, like someone ransacked a mining operation to get materials to shore up her rib cage. She is a fairly well-appointed individual, I must say.

In anticipation of… I don't know what, Tessa has lifted her left foreleg and is holding it for me. This is not exactly what I need her to be doing, though, but danged if her eagerness to please isn't just melting this old heart of mine.

I pull on my wading boots and splash into the water next to her. I'm not sure how to get her to drop her leg, but I give it a little tug—pointless, I realize—and then wade around to her other side and lean into her opposite forearm. Or whatever you want to call the long metal structure that acts as one of her main foundational points.

I don't think the leaning has any effect whatsoever, but the confused swing of her head as she tries to follow my movements causes her to feel the need to drop that leg back down. I figure once I start climbing up it, she'll understand that she's meant to keep it planted.

OK, crazy thing about this creature: she's got a way for me to climb up one of her front legs, but not the other one. So, after wrestling the first two sacrificial anodes into place on the first leg, I set in on the second one, only to realize I can't do it the same way. I end up using the rope and hooks to hold me in place from the top while I descend like a spider onto the uncooperative leg. By this time, Tessa's doing that weird moan and I'm really worried about the tide. I'll have to leave the other two legs for another day.

I pack up my gear, give her that obligatory pat on her skull-like head, and set out. An ache forms in the hollow of my chest as she tries to follow me. I chalk it up to all the physical movement I've been doing lately. I'm sure I've strained something.

You can never predict how things are going to turn out. I tried, day after day, to get back into the lagoon, but each day the water was too high, and there was no path. This was a disappointment, but what could I do but keep trying?

I thought about renting a boat, but I've never driven one, and if I rent *those* services, too, well, then, someone else is going to see Tessa, and that just won't do. It was an honest-to-goodness conundrum.

And then there was the problem of rabbit food.

I'm a real regimented guy. I tend to eat the same meals, walk the same roads, go to the same stores, and buy rabbit feed exactly every other week. So, of course, I find myself face-to-face with Tessa's keeper.

I am curious about this fellow. Anyone with the know-how and wherewithal to construct a giant, seemingly living creature has my respect and interest. I look around the feed store, like it might give me clues about the man who owns it. It's certainly neat, and clean, and well-stocked. He keeps his store in way better condition than he keeps his house, from what I've seen of it. Even the cage in the corner that contains a half-dozen week-old chicks is impeccably scrubbed and shining under a glowing heat lamp. But I don't see anything innovative or out-of-the-ordinary.

The feed store owner never has been much of a talker, and it seems things haven't changed. He does say, as he's ringing up my purchase, "I do appreciate you flying under the radar with… you know."

"She can be fixed," I say, hopefully.

He shakes his head. "She's got a terminal malfunction."

I don't ask what that is, or how it can happen in a metallic structure. I do notice that he doesn't touch my hand like he usually does when he gives me my change back. I notice, also, that it disappoints me.

The days stretch into weeks, and then into months. I learn that the man at the feed store has a name. It's Dennis. I don't learn anything else because I never ask, and I already know I'm skating on thin ice with the Tessa debacle. I want to go back and finish the job on her legs, but I'm worried that if I say a single word about her, I'll lose my opportunity. Somehow my access will be closed forever.

It may as well be anyway, though. I can find no favor with the tides for three full months and then, at last, on a walk that feels like it's bound to be as hopeless as all my others, the path is dry, and I can enter the lagoon.

The sun is warm and its reflection dances across the gentle ripples in the water. I can smell the scent from the pine forest high atop the cliff at the far end of the lagoon, the tallest trees looking like sentinels above this hidden place. What is this sensation in my heart? Happiness? I'm not sure I would know.

I tell myself not to rush, that maybe she won't

remember me, that I don't want to scare her. I try to prepare myself for her hind legs being quite a bit worse off than when I last saw her, and for her moans to be more pitiful and heart-tugging.

I had not thought to prepare myself for her to be gone.

It is not as if she can hide. She's damn near as big as the Golden Gate bridge. I mean, not really, but that's what jumps into my mind and, hyperbole or not, the comparison has an accurate feel to it.

Now I'm mad at Dennis. And mad at myself. Maybe I should have tried to talk to him. Maybe if I got to know him, he would come to trust me. Maybe we both could have helped Tessa.

But where did she go? Where could he have taken her?

I'm good at observing things—like I've said—and I'm pretty sure that if there had been a way out of here, I'd have seen it.

Well, maybe. Come to think of it, there have been a few times when I've missed things completely. Like when Dennis drove me out in his boat. It didn't feel like the same way I came in, and yet…. what other way is there?

I drop my pack onto the dry patch of land where I've been standing. I've been carrying that darn thing almost every day since I first brought it with me to work on Tessa. I stretch my back and have a look around.

And that's when I see it. The shape of something in the water, like the wrecked bones of an old ship come to rest against the walls of the lagoon.

I know it before I know it. That it's her.

I feel my chest cave in and dissolve in hot pain. I feel the volcanic rush of tears, as if my stomach is a pool of magma and every emotion I've ever suppressed over the last 50-odd years is bubbling out of me in a pyroclastic flow.

I suck in a breath of air and it turns into a choking sob.

I run, blindly, along a thin strip of sand—tripping and hitting the water, getting up, and running again.

When I reach her mostly submerged body, I splash into the water and follow her long, ridiculous neck to her bony head.

Her eyes are closed. Closed. As if that were even possible from obsidian shoved into metallic holes. As if any of this were possible.

She is gone. Whatever animating force fueled her motions when I first met her has vanished. She is nothing but an empty shell, and I have never felt so bereft in all my life.

I reach into the water and touch her head. I look at her submerged body, her legs curled and crumpled against her like a dead spider. I wonder if it would have made any difference if I had been able to get back to her sooner. And so what if it would have? It was an impossible task. But the thought of it deepens my suffering and the knot in my guts has me thinking I might vomit.

I don't know what Dennis meant by "terminal malfunction," but I wish he hadn't just left her here alone. I'd have stayed. I'd have spent her last days with her.

I think on that fact with wonder.

A million opportunities come along in a lifetime. A million opportunities to love and be loved, and I passed on nearly all of them. Looking down at the impossible creature in the water, I feel like I am submerged with her; I am finding it hard to breathe.

I backtrack out of the swaying water, and I don't even care that I can't see where I'm going because my eyes are filled with tears. I want to take her with me. I want to carry her home and dig an enormous hole and feel like I did something that mattered by laying her to rest close to me. But there's nothing I can do for her now. And maybe there never was.

I go back along the strip of sand to the tenuous beach and pick up my pack. It contains all the seemingly inconsequential things that gave my life meaning over the last few months. Now I won't need any of them. Won't even need to carry that pack around anymore. I'm trying to think what I'll do now, but the sun's light is bleeding on the water like the rust of a thousand wrecked ships and I don't even know how to stop crying.

I walk slowly out of the lagoon, feeling the drag of the water like a tug on my soul. I listen to the sucking sound of my wading boots in the wet sand and try to fathom that I don't need to come back here ever again.

When I reach the bottom of the street leading to my residence—and look past the rows of cheery pastel-painted houses—I feel, for the first time, a reluctance to go home. For just a moment, I stop. I slide the pack off my shoulders and look around me, like I'm seeing this town for the first time.

I have walked these streets for ages. I have made mental notes about every house, and fence, and dog, and lizard, and window-dressing. Yet now it all feels foreign, like I have just stepped off a plane in a land I don't yet know. The feeling of unfamiliarity is disconcerting. What do I do now? Where will I go? Who am I?

I have no idea.

I pick up my pack again and strike out in the direction of home. I'm not sure what that is anymore, but I guess I'll figure it out. Anyway, I have my rabbits to feed.

———

AUTHOR'S NOTE ON "HITCHING A SACRIFICIAL ANODE

TO A WELL-APPOINTED METAL MONSTROSITY"

I love how this story came about. I was in a creative writing class, working on the last assignment. I had NO inspiration! I had spent several months spooling out all the stories I already had in the works, and at the end I felt pretty dried up. I decided to do something unusual. I told myself that I would open up a dictionary to three random places. Whichever words my eyes fell upon would become part of the TITLE of my next story. The words I ended up with were: sacrificial anode (what the hell even WAS that?), hitch, and well-appointed. As I thought about those words, a story began to form in my mind. What I ended up with was "Hitching a Sacrificial Anode to a Well-Appointed Metal Monstrosity." The original story was written over the span of a day-and-a-half, and then I had to present it to my peers. I was filled with trepidation. Surely, they would find it ridiculous!

They did not. They loved it. I came to love it, too. In fact, it has become one of my favorite things I have ever written. Would it be weird to say that I still cry when I read it? Because I do.

About the Author

STARLENE JUSTICE is a Professor of Geography at Norco College in southern California. In addition to the pleasure she takes in teaching students about the world they live in, she adores writing. She will write anything. A sentence. A paragraph. A story.

A whole bloody novel. And she has done so.

Her first manuscript was finished at the tender age of 10. (It was not published). Her second manuscript was finished at the badass age of 12. (It, too, was not published—though it was better than the first!). Her third manuscript was completed at the age of 35. (Wait… did we lose time?) Her fourth manuscript was the thesis for her MFA in Creative Writing. "The Evangelist." It was self-published in 2019. Why stop there? Her self-published motivational title "The Astonishing Light of Your Own Being" dropped in 2020.

In the meantime…. *Newfound* published her non-fiction piece "The Thin Veil. *Strategy & Tactics* published her non-fiction piece "Geographic Determinism and the Russo-Japanese War." *Bosque* published her short story "Derailed." Hex Publishers selected her story, "The Scarlet Tanager" for inclusion in the anthology *Shadow Atlas: Dark Landscapes of the Americas*. This same story was nominated for a Pushcart Prize.

LINKS

Facebook: facebook.com/starlene.justice
Website: starlenejustice.com

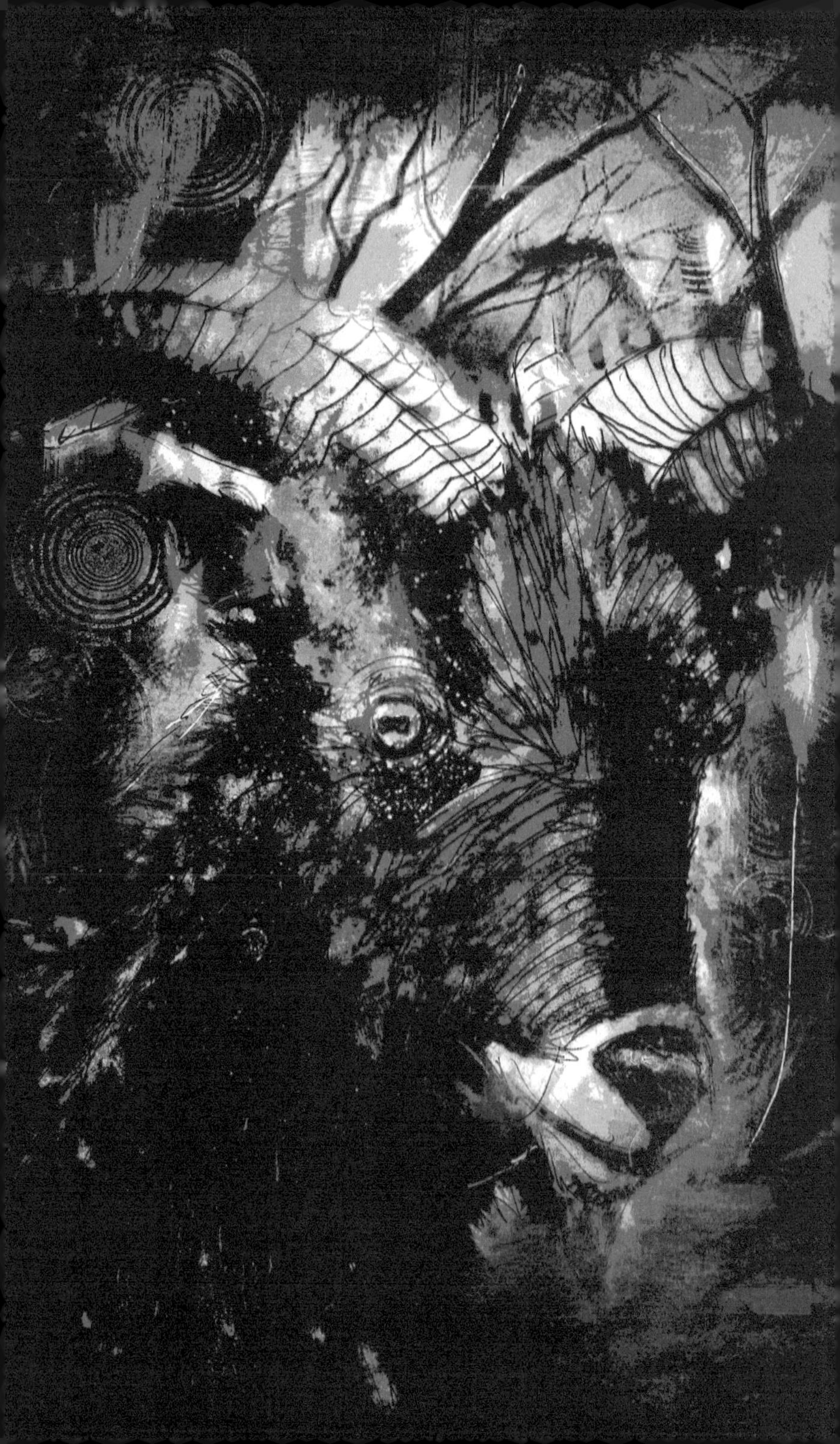

Honey, Blood, and Hellfire

by Matilda Lewis

My mother's name means sorrow. A cruel name for a child, to be sure, and a name that haunted her all her life, from the moment she came into the world blind, to the night she suffered my father's embrace, to the moment she bore me alone in the shadows of her blindness. The midwife wouldn't attend to her for fear that she would bring forth a monster. Even my uncle and his wife, who had grudgingly cared for her since the death of my grandparents, chose to spend the night in the barn, bedded down with the goats, rather than help deliver my mother of a demon's child.

I still remember the fear in my mother's voice when she told me the story of my birth.

I sat in her lap. Her arms were wrapped around me, holding me close as she spoke. Perhaps she worried that I would try to run away if I knew the truth. For a flicker of an instant, I had wanted to.

"I was afraid that I would have to kill you," my mother sighed against the crown of my head; it made me shudder. "But when I held you, I knew I couldn't. I felt your feet for hooves and found little toes. I felt your brow for horns and felt none. Your gums held no sharp teeth, nor did your mouth have a forked tongue…" She tightened the circle of her arms around me. I still remember how she smelled, like goatskin and coppery sweat and the wildflowers my aunt left hanging from the rafters to dry.

"When you cried, my milk came down and it didn't matter anymore what your father was." She kissed my hair. I felt her chest expand against my back as she breathed in the scent of it. I still remember how her words caught in her throat when she murmured, "You were *my* baby, too."

I was only six years old and I didn't understand what she meant, but my heart broke for my mother that day. I turned to face her and touched her freckled cheek. Even with her frown and the misting of her cloudy eyes, even with the cross-shaped scar on her forehead from where she'd been branded, my mother was beautiful. No one so beautiful should be so sad, I thought, but for as long as I could remember, my mother had always lived up to her name.

After I was born, the people of the town wouldn't let my mother join them for Mass. She tried to go with me, when I was only an infant, but before she could make it to the doors, she was met with insults and threats. Women who had braided her hair and crowned her with flowers when they were children told her she would burn and I would burn, too. Men who had watched her blossom into womanhood with guilty, unspoken longing called her a whore. She was no longer welcome in the house of God. Not alone, and not with me. Recounting the story, my uncle told me he had never feared so much for her. He had missed communion to take her back home and watch over her while she wept.

Still, the cruelty hurled against her never dimmed her faith. Still, my mother said her prayers. Sometimes, for hours, she knelt by the hearth with her head bowed and arms crossed over her chest, warmed by the fire as if it were the love of Christ.

One night, I remember curling up beside the hearth with a sickly kid goat my uncle had brought in for me to care for, when Father Ambrose came to pray with my mother and give her communion. He had come to visit her once a month as far back as my memory stretched; sometimes, I felt that I could almost remember, in a faint and hazy way, seeing him before I had been weaned off my mother's milk, before I could speak more than a few simple words. I wondered if my mother had ever let him hold me when I was a baby. Sometimes, I wished he would fold me in his arms the same way my mother did when I wanted for comfort or attention.

That night, I wondered if he sometimes wanted to, but held back for fear. I realized that he took a risk every time he stepped over our threshold. The people of the town would not approve of him giving communion to someone like my mother or being in the presence of someone like me, and I was sure their disapproval would spell danger for him if they found out.

Though Father Ambrose gave my mother communion, he did not do the same for me and never had—my mother was a child of God, but I was not. Not unbaptized as I was, not with a father such as mine. Though he gave me no sacraments, I never saw Father Ambrose as unkind for it and looked forward to his visits as much as my mother did. He brought her the holiness she longed for and had been denied. For me, he was pleasant company, still young enough to be handsome, with a soothing rhythm in his deep, soft voice.

Like he often did when he visited us, that night Ambrose brought me honeycomb from the hives he kept in the copse beside the churchyard. As always, I ate it—greedy for sweetness—though this time I couldn't help but wonder if the bees that made the honey fed on flowers mourners left on the graves.

While my mother prayed with Father Ambrose, I watched the fire dancing in the confines of the hearthstones. The sickly goat snuggled up beside me and rested her head in my lap. She had fallen asleep. I stroked her sides while she shivered, felt her ribcage expand and contract with each labored breath. I hoped against hope that she would survive the night and breathe easy one day.

The crackle and hiss of the fire muted the priest's voice as he spoke with my equally quiet mother, but I could still hear what they said if I focused on the sound.

"I remember what it was like to go a day without sorrow in my heart," my mother said, her voice pitched low. She must not have wanted me to hear her. I pretended not to listen. "It seems so long ago, but I remember. I had hoped it would be better by now."

"It will take time," replied Father Ambrose. "Wounds in the spirit take longer to heal than wounds on the body, but they do heal. First, we suffer, and then we heal. Then we know peace."

He stood and mother knelt at his feet. With the taste of honey on my tongue and the goat's soft white head in my lap, I watched the priest place the sacramental bread in my mother's mouth and saw how the tips of his fingers brushed against her bottom lip. I saw a hazy softness in his brown eyes as he watched her swallow the communion wine. That night, when Father Ambrose knelt in front of my mother and took her hands while they prayed together, something in his voice caught in his chest, low and thick.

Perhaps it was only a trick of the shadows cast by the hearth fire, but I swear I saw him tremble.

———●———————————————●———

Though I nursed her as best as I was able, the little goat I had hoped would recover from her sickness died not long after Father Ambrose's visit. My uncle grew ill not long after that, keeping us awake at night with his labored breathing, his moans and coughing. My aunt and my mother did what they could and so did I; we tried to keep him warm when he had chills, to cool him down when he broke into a sweat. I brewed him tea to soothe his ragged throat.

By the end, the fever had robbed him of all sense. He cried out in fear, he saw things that my aunt and I did not, heard things even my mother—whose hearing was keener than any of ours by virtue of having to rely on it more—could not hear. Demons in the shadows, demons in the light of the fire, shrieking and hissing and calling our names—my mother's, at least, and mine. My aunt would have sent us away, but even sick and afraid my uncle loved his sister and forbade his wife from driving us out.

The night before my uncle died, I pretended to

go to sleep early while I listened to him and his wife argue in the loft where they slept, their voices harsh and hushed. "We've done her wrong before," he rasped. "I can't let you do it again. Swear you won't blame them."

"Even the girl?" She couldn't bear to call me my name; I was always "the girl" to her.

"It would kill my sister." When my aunt did not respond, he pressed, "Promise me. Swear it."

I opened my eyes just enough to peer up and see her cross herself in the loft.

I saw the black goat for the first time the day we buried my uncle. While Father Ambrose prayed with my crying aunt and weeping mother, I caught a glimpse of the beast at the edge of the woods. He was bigger than our old Billy goat, with a heavier coat and longer horns. For the briefest moment, he inclined his shaggy head so his gaze met mine.

His eyes were beautiful and gold.

That night, I dreamed of following the black goat into the dark woods. The deeper into the forest I followed him, the tighter the gnarled weave of trees strangled the path until I could scarcely take a step without a branch catching me against my belly or my legs or the small of my back, leaving scratches and bruises.

In the morning, I woke with a stabbing ache in

the cradle of my hip bones and spots of brownish red dotting my thighs and the bed linen beneath me. Though my mother told me it wouldn't be long until I started bleeding and I knew to expect it soon, knowing wasn't enough to calm my silent panic.

"Does it always hurt?" I asked my aunt through my clenched teeth while she showed me what to do with blood moss and rags.

I saw her lack of pity clear in her red-rimmed eyes, the thin line of her mouth. I was certain she wished she hadn't promised my uncle on his deathbed that she would not throw me out. She was angry with me for daring to have a crisis of my own so soon after the death of her husband. For a moment, I wanted to tell her I wished it would have waited, too. A season, a year.

"Our Lord wouldn't have cursed Eve with it if it wasn't painful." The way she spoke without any hesitation at all chilled me, though I should have expected it. My aunt, who hadn't bled for years, scolded my mother as if she were a willful, wicked child whenever her blood came.

I wished I hadn't asked my aunt and wondered how my mother would have answered. She never seemed to hurt too badly during her time, or else she had gotten used to gritting her teeth and hiding her pain. In all my life, I could only remember her crying from it once, when she had spent an entire day in bed, curled in on herself beneath her quilt as she bled.

By the time the leaves had fallen and began to bud again, my aunt joined my uncle in the ground, victim to the same sickness and delirium that had killed her husband. My mother wept for her, though there had been little love between them. Privately, I was relieved my aunt had made it past the winter. I had been the one to dig her grave and it had been a trial that left me with painful, ugly blisters on my hands for days. I couldn't imagine how hard it would have been if the ground had frozen over, though it would have seemed fitting for her to give me trouble one last time with her death.

That summer, I went into town alone for the first time. All five of our nanny goats had given birth in the early spring—one to twins—and I intended to bring three of the kids to Father Ambrose to see if he would sell them for us. I didn't think anyone in town would take them if they knew who they belonged to.

I met Father Ambrose in the copse where he kept his hives. He must have heard me approach—I made no effort to muffle my steps and the goats heralded my approach with hoofbeats and bleating—but he did not turn away from the wax he was collecting. The church must have needed candles, I thought, but tried not to think about it for long. Whenever my mind turned towards the church, I remembered how my uncle said I could never go there, how my aunt told me I would burn if I set foot on consecrated ground. I dared go no farther than the beehives, and while there, I tried not to look in the direction of the rough chapel beyond the graveyard.

"You've brought friends, Melina?" Ambrose said, straightening. He held out a piece of honeycomb for me.

I stepped forward and accepted it with a nod that should have been a curtsy. "Just some goats. I was hoping you'd help me sell them." With one hand, I held out the goats' lead and with the other, I brought the honeycomb to my mouth. I savored its sweet taste and swallowed. "I don't have friends."

Father Ambrose took the lead from me. "You have your mother," he said. He turned his gaze down, as if ashamed of the warmth in his dark eyes. "You have me."

I licked honey from my fingers and stared at him, my eyes narrowing. "Do you love my mother?"

"You should get back to her. I'll see about selling your goats."

───

After my aunt's death, I took to sleeping in her bed in the loft instead of beside my mother in her bed by the hearth. More and more often, I had dreams that woke me in the night, sometimes afraid and sometimes aflame in a way that felt unseemly, embarrassing.

Through spring and summer, my mother wasn't bothered by my nightly absence but once the autumn chill set in, she called for me to sleep in her bed, complaining of the cold.

"The fire isn't warm enough," she said, almost pleading. Her face was turned in my direction, but her sightless eyes couldn't find me. "Come sleep next to me."

"I will, tonight."

"Until it warms up again?"

I peeled back the quilts and crawled into bed beside her. My foot brushed her cold shin. "Until I can find another blanket for you."

"Is it really so awful?" She reached out to me, gave my shoulder a squeeze when she found it. A kiss followed.

"No." I nestled back against her. "It's not."

For a long moment, neither of us spoke. I listened to my mother breathing next to me and set the rhythm of my breath against hers. I could feel her heartbeat against my back; mine kept time with hers.

"I miss when you were little, sometimes," she sighed, in a tone like the one I heard when she confessed her sins.

"Because I never minded sleeping next to you?"

"It was nice having someone to care for," she said. "Nobody had ever needed me before."

I didn't know what she wanted me to say. Did she want to hear I needed her still? She would know it was a lie. My mother needed me far more than I needed her, to keep up with all the work her blindness prevented her from doing. I chopped and hauled wood for our hearth, I set and checked traps, I fed the goats, I tended the garden, I mended our clothes, I did most of the cooking and tidying. My mother could scrub linens, knead dough, milk goats, and card wool, but without the use of her eyes there was only so much she could do. Without me, she would freeze. Without me, she would starve. I could tell her all of that but didn't want to. She already knew. It didn't matter, anyway; I loved her.

After a long moment, a question formed unbidden in my mind. Desperate for an answer, I asked, "Mama, do you think I'm wicked?"

"No—I don't know," she murmured. I couldn't tell if she was still awake or half-asleep. "I don't *care*."

———•———

I saw the black goat again the day of the first snowfall. He stood at the edge of the forest, dark as spilled ink. Dark as rot on grain.

I was sure he was watching me. He fixed me with his golden, unblinking gaze.

"What do you want?" I called out. With a snort, he turned to trot past the tangled threshold of the woods. I followed.

He should've been easy to keep in sight, dark as he

was against the whiteness of the snow, but I soon lost track of him. I feared losing the path, and had made up my mind to head back when I heard a woman singing just a little deeper into the woods.

Her voice was velvety and warm. I didn't know what language she sang in, but it was lovelier than anything I had ever heard.

I pushed aside a bramble and stepped into a clearing I hadn't known existed. The woman sat on a fallen tree, wearing a black dress and a black riding cloak, both edged in gold. Her boots were black, too, with gold spurs. Her tumbling hair was black as well, and when she lifted her eyes to look at me, her eyes were as gold as the goat's eyes—gold as honey.

She was so beautiful, looking at her made my teeth hurt. It took me a long time to find my voice. When I did, it wavered. "Who are you?"

Her wry smile hid her teeth but the light in her eyes was mirthful. "Your father," she said.

"You're a woman."

She shifted on her perch and examined her tapered nails. "When it suits me."

"What do you want?"

Her lips formed a comely pout. "I only wanted to see my daughter. The last time I was this close to you was when I drew you from your mother."

My stomach turned. "That's a lie. My mother was alone when she gave birth to me."

"Is that what she told you, then?" The smile

remained upon the woman's mouth, but it had left her eyes. She cocked her head like a crow sizing up something dead. "She was delirious from exhaustion, poor thing. Fear, too, I'd wager."

She didn't give me time to respond before she spoke again. "You've grown lovely; you'll grow lovelier still…" I could feel her gaze on me, sweet and sticky. I liked it, though I knew I shouldn't.

Taken by a different thought, the woman asked, "Do you like my clothes? I could get you something like them, in any color you pleased."

The notion of owning something so fine sent a chill of delight down my back, but I shook my head. "I wouldn't have anywhere to wear them or anyone to see them."

"A secret? Even better."

I stepped backwards until my shoulders met the bramble. "I have to go home."

"I won't stop you. Go on."

On my way out of the woods, I heard the woman's song again, though I wasn't sure if she was singing aloud or if her voice was in my head.

⬤━━━━━━⬤

While the people in the town were preparing for Christmas, my mother prayed even more than was her custom. Every so often, I thought of interrupting her, just to have someone to talk to, just so I could hear her say something other than another prayer I feared would go as unanswered as the rest.

On the longest night of the year, a knock on the door interrupted her prayers before I had the chance.

"Who's there?" she called. From my vantage point in the loft, I saw her twist, tense-shouldered, towards the door. I set aside the holly crown I'd been weaving and scrambled down the ladder.

I heard Father Ambrose answer, his voice muffled by the winter wind. He had come earlier this month to give my mother communion and take her confession, so we weren't expecting him. Still, I opened the door to let him in. His cheeks and nose were red from the cold. He seemed in high spirits as he brushed snowflakes from his dark, curly hair.

"What brings you, Father?" my mother asked. She pulled her shawl tight, shivering.

He unfastened his heavy cloak and shrugged it off his shoulders. "I thought you and Melina might be lonely." He folded the garment and draped it over the nearest chair. A leather flask hung against his hip, which he removed and offered to me.

Gingerly, I accepted it. I cradled it to my chest.

"Honey mead," Ambrose explained when he recognized the questioning look on my face. "For your mother. It's a little strong for you, yet."

When he turned his attention to my mother, I snuck a swig. It was sweet, but the burn of it made me sputter and cough.

Until then, I had never heard Father Ambrose laugh. I hadn't imagined it possible, but even if I had, I wouldn't have imagined his laughter would sound so bright, so warm. "I warned you."

Shamed, I brought the flask to my mother.

She brought it to her lips and took a dainty sip. "Thank you."

With slow, stiff movements, Father Ambrose knelt next to my mother. "It's a cold night. I thought you might like something to warm you up."

"She has the fire, Father." *And me.*

My mother took another sip of mead. "Hush, Lina."

For the rest of the evening, I did. After a while, I retreated to the loft and to my half-finished holly crown. I turned my focus to weaving the bright-berried sprigs together. The murmur of my mother and Father Ambrose speaking with one another faded away to a soft hum.

It was only when two words, pitched low—*I'm sorry*—found their way to my ears that my hands stilled, and I raised my head to peer down at my mother and the priest.

He traced the lines of the scar on her forehead with his thumb. "I would never have done this to you," I heard him say. "Never."

He pressed a kiss to her scar, as chaste as she kissed my scrapes when I was little, after I put her fingers to the hurt.

The kiss my mother gave Ambrose in return was not as chaste. She brought her hand to his cheek and kissed him on the mouth.

He took her hand and pulled away.

I could not hear what it was he said to her before he left.

When I came down from the loft to take my place beside my mother for the night, I said nothing to her. Wordless, I peeled back the quilts.

"You don't have to," she said, her voice thick. "It's warm enough tonight."

I let the quilts drop. "If you say so."

That night as I tried to sleep, I heard my mother sigh alone in her bed.

———

A long and lonely winter passed. Without my aunt and uncle to share the burden of all the work there was to be done, it was harder than any winter I could remember. Still, we survived, my mother and I. I kept our hearth warm, and we had enough to eat, though I had to butcher our oldest goat. I hated doing it, but her milk had dried up. While the other four grew fat with the kids they'd deliver in the spring, the oldest had gone barren and my mother doubted that she would breed successfully next year.

We ate like queens the day after I killed the goat, but it was hard to enjoy the meal with the memory of her beautiful golden eyes upon me. She had trusted me even as I stepped towards her with a knife in my hands.

———————●———————

The summer of my sixteenth year was stormy and hot. Dark clouds roiled in the sky and I could smell rain coming as I made my way to the creek with my laundry basket against my hip. Last summer, it had been harder to balance, but over the year I'd grown into a body less like a boy's and more like my mother's.

Sometimes, when I saw myself reflected in calm water, I remembered the honey-sweet words of the golden-eyed woman in the woods: *You've grown lovely,* she said. *You'll grow lovelier still.* When I felt most vain, I imagined myself wearing the fine clothes she had offered me. My brief delight at the thought shamed me every time.

When I reached the creek, I wasn't surprised to find myself alone. But for the gathering storm, other people would have been by the water's edge, washing clothes like me, maybe fishing or in the water swimming. It was better no one else was around; I didn't have to face their glaring eyes and unkind whispers.

I made quick work of the laundry, the smocks and chemises and bloodstained sheets, and I hummed the tune I had heard my father sing in the woods. I would have sung the song, but I couldn't remember the words, not in the strange language that had spilled from my father's lips. Every so often, I paused to wipe the sweat from my brow or the back of my neck.

When I had scrubbed everything clean, I folded it all and piled it in my basket. The storm hadn't broken and I had time before I needed to return home. I cast a glance around me to be certain I was still alone and then I knelt to take off my boots and stockings. I hiked my skirt up to my knees and stepped into the water.

The gentle rush cooled my heated skin. Though the smoothness of the rocks beneath my toes was pleasant, it was treacherous, too. It was with great care that I waded deeper into the creek, lifting my skirt to match the rising level of the water until it flowed around my thighs. I stood still with the taste of the coming rain in my mouth and listened to the low, far-off rumble of thunder and the sighing of the breeze. I closed my eyes and wondered if it was like this for my mother—no harsh light, no garish colors to distract from the feeling of water or the sound of a distant storm.

There is nothing more beautiful than this, I thought. *Nothing.*

A man's voice broke into my daydream. "I said, does that feel good?"

Startled, I nearly slipped. When I caught my balance, I saw him on the opposite side of the creek from where I had come. He was a little older than me, with fair hair and a crooked smile. The look in his eyes reminded me of how Father Ambrose gazed at my mother when he didn't know I was watching him, but warped and wrong—all heat, no warmth.

He took a step towards the creek's edge, and I took a step back. "Aren't you worried about the storm coming?"

I took another step backwards. His heavy footsteps made a splash in the creek. "I've never seen you in the town before."

"You wouldn't have."

"That's a pity." The young man advanced, heedless of the water that soaked through his shoes and breeches.

I shook my head. "No, no, it's not." By the time I felt grass on the soles of my feet, I was ready to abandon my things and run if I had to. "I promise it's not."

"Why so skittish? I don't mean you any harm."

As I was about to flee, I heard a voice calling my name, deep and sweet. I dared look away from the fair-haired man to see a hunter approaching with a musket at his shoulder and dead rabbits hanging from his belt. Gold glinted in his eyes.

The young man stopped in the middle of the creek and came no closer to me, but I could feel his gaze upon my back as I walked away from him with the hunter at my side.

•————————•

In the following days, my thoughts drifted often to the fair young man. A glance into the golden eye of the goat I was milking made me think of the gold of his hair. When I fetched water from the well, the splash of the bucket brought to mind the splash of his boots in the creek.

Sometimes, when it was dark and I lay awake in the loft, I wondered what it would've been like if I had let him near me. He said he hadn't meant me any harm—what if he had been telling the truth? I wondered what it would be like to run my fingers through his hair, to let him kiss me or put his hands upon me. Sometimes, when I couldn't sleep, I imagined what might have happened if I hadn't run away. It built an ache in me where once I'd only ached when I bled. Like a loose milk tooth, it begged to be prodded at and soothed with a touch. It left me feeling ashamed—sometimes ashamed enough to cry—soon after I was done and I was certain it was a sin, but it felt so needful and so good it made me almost grateful to have been damned already.

Still, guilt hounded me. I thought of telling my mother about the young man at the creek, but every time I felt the words rising up like bile, I swallowed them back down. I wouldn't want to worry her.

As a little girl, I had never kept secrets from her. Now, between the fair young man, my father, and Father Ambrose, I had three. I didn't like how they felt, slick and heavy, writhing like snakes.

When the leaves turned the colors of fire and the summer heat gave way to the crisp chill of autumn, I started sharing my mother's bed with her again.

"I never got you that blanket," I said, close to sleep. When I looked over my shoulder at her, I saw she'd closed her cloudy eyes and her jaw had gone slack. I curled up next to her and drifted off.

When I woke, the roses of dawn had yet to bloom and my mother's side of the bed was empty. The hearth had cooled to embers.

"Mama?" No answer. I sat upright and blinked sleep from my eyes as they adjusted to the darkness. Though the light of the moon spilled in from the window, none of the shadows it cast were shaped like my mother. Panic tightened my chest as I threw back the quilts and scrambled out of bed. Without so much as finding a shawl to wrap around my shoulders, I grabbed the lantern and went outside to search for my mother. I thought of the fair young man at the creek and of my father. My stomach twisted.

"Mama?" I called.

No answer—not from her.

Beside the barn, the black goat emerged from the darkness. He trotted off into the woods and I followed.

When I crossed into the trees, the hunter waited for me. He pressed a finger to his lips and held out his hand for me to take. I clasped it and let him lead me along the path to the clearing in the woods where I encountered him in the shape of the singing woman. Silent, he gestured towards his eyes with two fingers, then flicked them in the direction of the opposite side of the clearing to draw my attention to the figures there, moving in the shadows.

At first, I thought Ambrose was forcing my mother—he had her pinned on her back in the moss and covered her mouth with one hand while he fucked her—but then I realized she wasn't fighting him, wasn't crying or trying to push him off of her. Her arms rested above her head, crossed at the wrists as if he'd held her down like that just moments before. She gripped his sides with her legs and dug her heels into the small of his scarred back, tight enough that I could see how the muscles in her pale calves tensed. I heard her muffled moans. Though from the darkening bruises on her hip and thigh, I could tell Ambrose had not been gentle with my mother; there was a tenderness in his voice when he sighed her name, when he called her lovely and sweet.

My face burned. I couldn't breathe. I looked away, into my father's eyes. For the first time, his smile showed his teeth. They were white and sharp and there were far too many of them. "You see?" he said. "I only gave your mother what she wanted."

He laughed, low and rumbling, at my distress.

Stumbling over roots and brambles, I fled. Back

home, back to the embers in the hearth. I don't remember when I fell asleep, but when I woke, it was in the early dawn light with my mother beside me breathing steadily in her sleep.

———•———

After that night in the woods, I saw my mother differently. I knew my aunt would have condemned her, called her a whore, and maybe worse. The people of the town would have done likewise. I couldn't—not even after seeing how roughly she'd let herself be treated. What I had seen should have made me sick, should have turned me away from her. I wondered if that was what my father had wanted—to turn me away from her.

If that was what he had meant to do, he failed. Now, when I saw her wipe her eyes with her sleeve so her welling tears wouldn't fall into the dough she kneaded, I understood a little more what made her cry. Once, I had thought it was the same loneliness that I felt when I gave myself time to dwell. Or perhaps it was due to some guilt, perhaps mourning for the life she might have had if she hadn't given birth to me, if she hadn't drawn my father's attention. If she hadn't been born blind.

I understood now that she wept for love, that to her it was worth sinning for.

———•———

When Father Ambrose came next to take my mother's confession and give her communion, I watched the two of them from my bed while I pretended to have gone to sleep early. They prayed and spoke so quietly I could hardly hear them over the crackle of the hearth fire and the moaning of the wind. I saw my mother's hands curl to fists, her bare feet tense against the floorboards as if holding back an impulse to go to the priest and draw him close. Ambrose winced when he moved, and I saw the rigid restraint in his arms. I couldn't reconcile the man I had seen in the woods—coarse and domineering— with the man lit by the hearth fire who kept his gaze low and couldn't look my blind mother in her face for longer than a moment. I had seen him timid before, but never so much as this.

After a prolonged silence, my mother reached out to the priest. His shoulders stiffened when her hand found his knee.

"Come away with us," I heard my mother say, her voice raised just enough for me to make out the words. "You don't have to stay here."

Ambrose brushed her hand aside as he stood to leave. After he bid my mother goodbye, I clambered down from the loft and threw my shawl about my shoulders.

My mother turned her face away from the fire towards me, her cloudy eyes red-rimmed. "I didn't know you were awake."

"I woke up. Have to piss." I opened the door and stepped outside.

Father Ambrose wasn't so far down the path that he'd disappeared from my sight, but I still had to sprint to catch up. "Wait!"

He stopped and turned to face me. My lungs burned while I panted and caught my breath. Ambrose said nothing, but I could see his confusion clear in the furrowing of his brow.

"Leave with us," I said. The words spilled out of my mouth like a swarm of bees, buzzing and frantic and stupid. "My mother loves you. Leave with us, go somewhere far away where nobody would know you or her. Nobody would know the truth. We'd be happy."

"You know I can't, Lina." The moon gave off just enough light for me to see how tired he looked, how unwell.

"Nobody would know she's not your wife and I'm not your daughter. She's not too old to give you a child. Please. You love her—I know you do. It's not fair that you're kept apart. It's not right. Nobody would know, if we went far enough away."

I reached out to grab his sleeve, to beg, but he drew back, wincing as if I burned him. His lip curled back in a snarl, wolfish, for a moment angry, and then his expression softened, and the warmth found its way back into his dark eyes—eyes, I saw then, that were very much like my own.

"Our Lord would know."

"But you would be happy!" I wiped at my tearing eyes with the heel of my hand; I didn't know why I was crying, but I couldn't stop. My shame at weeping only made my nose run harder and tears flow faster. "I swear you would."

"Lina…" Ambrose pulled me close and let me cry against his chest as if he were my father. His heart beat against the side of my face, quick and unsteady. I could smell his sweat and feel the comforting warmth of his body. His voice was low and measured when he hushed me. "I would be happy, but it would be a sin. A grave sin."

He drew back and stooped so his eyes were level with mine. "You know that, don't you?"

I knew but I wanted to scream that it didn't matter, that I didn't care, that no matter how much Christ had sacrificed for him and every other sinner—my mother loved him more. I knew that, I had seen how much in the quiet moments by the hearth and in the moss and shadow of the woods. I wanted to tell him so much that my throat burned with the words I bit back. I couldn't bear to remind him I was my father's daughter. Not his.

I let him leave without another word. With bleary eyes, I watched him disappear into the darkness along the path.

On the walk back home, I spied the black goat in the brambles, spying on me with his golden eyes, and I spat on the ground in front of him.

That night, Father Ambrose appeared in my dreams, standing at the edge of the woods, gaunt and hollow-faced. He showed me deep punctures in his wrists. The wounds bled honey that rolled down his hands and dripped, thick and gold, from his fingertips. I knelt before him like my mother did when he gave her communion. Sad-eyed, he shook his head and stepped away from me, into the darkness of the woods behind him.

As I'd once followed the black goat, I followed Father Ambrose as he led me deeper and deeper into the gloom. The further I walked, the further he slipped away until I lost him completely, and I was alone in the branch-haunted silence. I searched and called out his name, but I couldn't find him, and he did not answer.

I shuddered awake in the pitch-black loft. My breathing was ragged; sweat plastered my hair to my brow. As my eyes adjusted, I caught a glint of golden eyes and sharp white teeth in the corner—just for an instant—and woke my mother with my scream.

The moon disappeared and grew full and waned again to nothing. In that time, Father Ambrose did not visit us. Without him, my mother wept more often, prayed more fervently.

"I never should have asked him to leave with us," she said one night over another supper she barely touched. "He must be furious."

I couldn't tell if the bitterness in her voice was regret for her actions, or anger at mine. She knew what I'd done, I was sure of it, but I couldn't muster the courage to apologize. I wondered if she blamed me more than herself. If I had not run after him and begged where my mother had only asked, perhaps he wouldn't have avoided us. He wouldn't have left my mother without communion or confession, and she would not have had to weep and pray for fear of sickness in the soul—or for loneliness, or for the loss of the man she loved.

For the first time I could remember, my mother's blindness was a relief to me; it meant she couldn't see shame blooming hot on my face or my shaking hands. I wanted to say something to comfort her, but couldn't find the words. I ate my bread in silence and watched her supper go almost untouched, again.

* * *

Another month passed, and Father Ambrose still had not come for my mother. No matter how I chided her—as if I were the mother and she a stubborn child—she refused to eat as she should. Flesh fell away from her hips and breasts first, then her belly, and finally her face. The glow of the hearth had once made her look radiant, but now only threw into starker relief the new hollowness in her cheeks and the shadows around her eyes. This was the first time I could remember being afraid for her. She wept for the state of her soul but the frailness of her body frightened me most. Though it was still warm outside, she shivered next to me in bed, even if I held her. I was only a little taller than her now, but she felt so small and I hated it.

One morning, when the rose-gold dawn spilled down upon my mother as she prayed, I could bear it no longer.

"I'm going into town," I said as I laced up my boots. "I'll bring Father Ambrose back with me."

My mother protested, but only weakly. She didn't try to stop me as I left.

Nervousness gnawed at my chest, a trapped animal that grew more frenzied the nearer I got to the church whose stones and steeple I still couldn't bear to look at. I hoped to find Ambrose by his hives, that I wouldn't have to ask someone to fetch him from inside the church.

I stepped into the copse beside the churchyard. There was a priest beside the beehives with his back to me, but it wasn't Ambrose. This man was smaller, with wheat-colored hair cropped close to his scalp.

I thought of the young man by the creek. The twisting and scratching behind my ribs spread down into my belly, hollowing me out from the inside. Even when the priest turned around and I saw his solemn, heavy-eyed face was so different from the fair young man's, I felt fear make a den of me.

"How can I help you?" he asked when he noticed me watching him. If I had startled him, he didn't show it. "You look lost." His voice was cold and reedy, so unlike the deep, warm voice of the priest I knew and the man my mother loved.

"I need to speak to Father Ambrose."

The priest bowed his head, frowning. "Ambrose has been dead of fever for weeks, it grieves me to say. He was well-loved here."

"Dead?" A low sob built in my chest. I couldn't hold back my tears. Who would take my mother's confession now? Who would give her communion, and keep her from the pits of Hell when she died? Who would keep her company when mine wasn't enough?

Even knowing what I was, Father Ambrose would have taken me in his arms to comfort me. He would have let me cry against his chest. This priest looked away, silently recoiling from my grief. To him I was just a girl like any other. He offered me nothing—not a kind word, not a gentle hand.

———•———

After learning of Father Ambrose's death, I often dreamed of the priest disappearing into the woods. Most nights, I woke in the still-dark early morning to catch a glimpse of the black goat, or the singing woman, or the hunter in the corner of the loft or at the foot of my mother's bed. I hated it now that it was in my home, watching my mother and watching me, perhaps emboldened by the priest's absence.

The first time I had seen it in the corner, on the night I had dreamed of Father Ambrose bleeding honey, it had vanished in an instant. It lingered now and it petrified me in my bed. I couldn't run away and couldn't fight it off, couldn't scream for fear or anger. I couldn't so much as whimper or curl a finger.

One morning, I went into the woods to see if I could find my father amongst the shadows of the gnarled trees whose leaves by now had shriveled and gone brown wherever they still clung to the branches. I spent hours searching, but found no trace—not of the black goat, nor the singing woman, nor the hunter.

I couldn't even find the clearing from before, where I had first seen my father and where it had showed me my mother with Father Ambrose. It was lost to me, though I had been certain I knew the way.

———————

My mother started eating again. At first it gave me hope, but as the nights grew longer and colder, I could tell the weeks without enough food had weakened her and left her fragile. She prayed incessantly, but where it had once filled her with a desperate energy, her recitation was hollow now, listless.

Still, she prayed. She prayed and shivered—even during the day now. Even with her shawl wrapped around her shoulders, even with a blanket. She scarcely had the energy to live, so her few remaining chores fell to me along with everything else.

I didn't complain. I was grateful for the distraction of work, of being too busy during the day and too tired at night to think for very long. Unlike my mother, I did not have the comfort of prayer. I hadn't the faintest hope that God would hear *my* prayers. Even if He did, why would He care about a demon's daughter and her grief?

No, not grief. It wasn't sorrow I was afraid of losing myself to. My mother grieved, my mother wept, but I did not. *I* was angry. I boiled and seethed and I wasn't sure whether I was angry with Father Ambrose or the God who compelled him to scourge himself for shame and then let him die from his rotting wounds, or if I was angry with myself for whatever role I had played in driving him away. No matter how hard I tried to keep it down, rage kept bubbling up in the back of my throat.

My teeth throbbed in their sockets as I clenched my jaw to trap my anger inside my mouth.

The leaves had fallen and my mother was dying slowly. It had started with the shivering, the fever followed, and then came the coughing. It was an ugly cough, deep and hacking, that spattered the crook of her elbow with blood. Sometimes, she was so weak that she couldn't lift a crust of bread to her mouth, so I cared for her like a child.

Though her body was failing her, her mind was clear. For her sake, I wish that it had not been. If her mind hadn't been so clear, she might not have been so afraid of dying, of what would happen to her after she was dead.

"He comes to me every night now, your father," my mother said one morning while I helped her put on a clean shift. "He lays on me until I can't breathe. He touches me. He pries my mouth open and sticks his fingers in until it makes me gag."

I didn't know what to say, so I said nothing. I circled behind her. With trembling hands, I braided her long hair. There were grey strands now, mixed in with the copper, duller now than it had once been.

"Sometimes he sounds like Ambrose. Like Ambrose, but wrong, Lina. I don't understand his language. It buzzes."

I hushed her, crooning like I would to soothe a nervous animal, like she had cooed and sighed to me when I was a child. I tied off her plait with a strip of cloth.

"It buzzes—" A coughing fit wracked her frame

before she could continue. When she caught her breath and wiped the blood and spit from her lips, she spoke again, "It buzzes in my head like a swarm of bees."

"With Father Ambrose's voice?"

"Yes," she said. "He spoke with Ambrose's voice once before, in my dream the night—the first night—" Another violent coughing spell, bloodier than the last, bent her double. When she recovered, my mother leaned back against me, too exhausted to hold herself upright. "He *was* Ambrose, in my dream."

I rubbed her bare arms and let her rest her head against my collarbone, as much to soothe myself as to calm her. She had never told me before that my father had come in the image of the priest the night it had forced itself on her. I wondered how, after that, she could stand to hear the real man's voice, to feel his touch and let him hold her down in the moss. I knew she loved him and suffered for it, but until she told me that secret, I had never known how much. I could not imagine loving someone whose voice—however soft and deep and lovely—reminded me of such horror.

"I saw you with Father Ambrose in the woods," I said. I kept my voice gentle, so she would know I wasn't accusing her. I hid my pity as best I could. "How could you bear it? He wasn't gentle with you, mama. He wasn't."

She didn't react with surprise, and I wondered if it was because she knew I had seen them in the woods or if she hadn't the vitality left for shock. She seemed not to have the life left for lies or denial either; she answered me straight away, "He wasn't like your father. He was—he only did what I asked." Another hacking cough. "He let go of me when I asked. If I was afraid."

I didn't know what to think or how to feel, torn between revulsion and care. I didn't want to dwell on it, and asked, "What do you think my father is trying to tell you?"

"I don't know." She began to cry. "I'm afraid."

———

By the day that the first snowflakes fell from the leaden winter sky, my mother could no longer hold herself upright. She couldn't speak except to murmur a word of a prayer or cry out in fear when her coughing let up. I tried to make her comfortable, brought her blankets and minded the fire when she shivered. I brought her water to drink and wet rags to cool her brow when her fever burned her despite the chill in the air. I sang songs she liked and told stories she had once told me.

More than once, I was tempted to pray for my mother's soul—it seemed too late to pray for her life. I knew God would not listen. Not to me. I couldn't save my mother from the hellfire we both feared awaited her.

"Ambrose?" Her voice was so hoarse I barely recognized it. Her eyes rolled in their sockets, searching blindly for him in the shadows cast by our hearth fire.

"He's gone, mama."

"No." She shuddered. "He wouldn't leave me."

"Mama, he's *dead.*"

She knew she would be dead soon, too. It was no longer a matter of days, but of hours, and Father Ambrose was not there to give her the final sacraments of her life.

With coos and teary-eyed promises, I left my mother's bedside to go into town and find the priest, to beg him to come for her. When I found him outside the church and told him my mother was dying, and begged that he come give her the final rites before death, his lip twisted into a sneer.

"That whore? Father Ambrose wouldn't have whipped himself to death if not for her. Let her get what she earned." With a dismissive wave, he turned from me and left to enter the church where I couldn't follow him. Even if I begged and screamed until I lost my voice, I knew from the cold iron in his eyes that he would never listen to me.

Too numb to cry, I returned home to my mother where she lay dying in the bed where my father had raped her, where she had given birth to me.

—•—

I dug my mother's grave out of frozen ground. My tears turned to ice on my cheeks and my hands blistered, then bled. I tried to remember her as she had been—sorrowful, yes, but beautiful, gentle, and kind.

I couldn't. No matter how many times I pushed the memory of her last moments down in the depths of my mind, it came bobbing back up like something dead in the water. I remembered how I held her hand, felt how sharp the bones of her fingers were. How her breath rattled in her chest. How she asked if the priest was coming.

How I lied and said he was.

●————————————————●

After my mother's death, I never saw my father again. Not in the shape of the black goat, nor the singing woman, nor the hunter. Perhaps it thought it had wrung all the suffering it could from us, like blood wrung from a soiled sheet until it was clean again. Once, as a little girl by the fire with a sickly goat resting her head in my lap, I had overheard Father Ambrose tell my mother that suffering eventually brings healing and peace—I understand now he was trying to assure himself it was true. I hope with all my heart that for him it is. I hope for my mother it is.

I hope it will be for me.

The moon hides behind the clouds. I can see my

breath turn silver against the darkness and I shiver, but I don't feel the cold. Not really.

I don't think I'll ever feel the cold again.

The church looms before me. Looking up from the bottom step, I see for the first time why someone would find its stones and stained glass beautiful, but it is the jeering gargoyles that draw my eyes. One has a face that reminds me of my father.

I gaze for a long moment into the stone hollows of its eyes. I can almost imagine them gold as a goat's eyes, gold as honey.

I spit on the ground between my feet and make my way up to the great carved door.

I pause with my hand upon the cold wood. If I go inside, I will burn. My clothes and hair will catch first, and then my flesh; I know my skin will bubble and blacken, and I am sure it will be agonizing until even the part of me that feels pain has burned away. My eyes will boil in their sockets. If I step inside this church, the flames will consume me until there is nothing left of me but bones and teeth and ashes.

I know I will burn, but what is left for me in life but ashes? I turn my head to look one last time at the veiled moon. Then, I push the door open, and step inside.

The church is empty and dark, barely warmer than the snow outside. My heart beats wildly in the hollow space in my chest as I wait for the flames, but I do not catch fire. I take another step forward but still nothing. With every step I take towards the altar, my trembling grows more violent.

The first spark catches on the wooden bench to my right. The flame smolders at first, then ignites in a bloom of light and heat. To my left, another flower blazes to life. Flames leap from bench to bench before me until the altar catches as I draw closer to it.

The church is in full bloom, but the fire leaves me untouched. My clothes catch; I can smell them burning on my body, but my body doesn't burn. With every flicker of the flames surrounding Him, the carved God above the altar seems in turns to sneer at me in revulsion and then to gaze down upon me with such compassion the pain on his contorted face seems to mirror my own sorrow, anger, and fear.

I stare up at Him, weeping. He doesn't burn, either, though the blaze engulfs the cross he hangs from as the fire spreads. Transfixed, I watch as I am judged, absolved, found guilty, and found innocent in His painted eyes.

Wood burns, glass shatters; over the infernal roar, the sound of people waking in a panic.

I had entered the church believing in my heart that I would be reduced to ash, but unburnt and unharmed, I realize that no matter how much I had wanted to die when I pushed open those cold doors, I don't want *them* to kill me.

Heedless of the smoke and heat, I make my way through the fire to the nearest window. The colored glass has broken and the lead warped enough that I can clamber out through it. On the ground outside, I drop to my hands and knees and use the snow to quell the flames smoldering on my clothes. Then I run.

I run through the graveyard where Ambrose must be buried, where my mother should have been buried beside him. I run through the copse, past the hives, all the way to the empty cottage I know can never be home to me again. My lungs ache, my legs ache, I nearly collapse upon the floor when I cross the threshold, though I know I cannot rest for long. Not here.

I slip out of my ruined bodice, skirt, and chemise and let them fall to the dirt floor. I open the chest where I kept our clothing. Folded tidily on top are my mother's clothes; I should have burnt them after she died, but I hadn't been able to bear the thought of watching the last part of her that remained in the world reduced to ash. I clutch her chemise to my bare chest, run my fingers along the tattered seams, smell the sickly perfume of death that still clings to the cloth, however faintly. One day, I might find a stream pure enough to wash it out.

I dress in my mother's old clothes and heavy cloak. I gather what I can carry in a pack and step over the threshold into the snow.

Before I leave, I open the door to the goats' barn. I can't take them with me, but maybe they'll find their way somewhere safe on their own if I let them go free.

Though my breath clouds in silver plumes in front

of me as I set off into the winter night, I'm not cold. I feel the heat from the church burning inside me. Where I step, the snow melts. My tears turn to steam on my face.

I risk one last glance back at my home—one final look at my mother's grave. Stumbling over the words, I whisper my first prayer.

With the same breath, I swear it will be my last.

***

AUTHOR'S NOTE ON "HONEY, BLOOD, AND HELLFIRE"

I often get my initial inspiration for a story from a song; "Honey, Blood, and Hellfire" is one of those stories. I had written a pair of short stories featuring Father Ambrose, Lina's mother, and Lina's demon father and liked the characters enough that I planned to revisit them at some point. The mood struck after I heard the song "I like the devil" by Purity Ring—a favorite band of mine. The narrator of the song details her mother's sorrow with a deep compassion, but also there's a sense of frustration towards the limiting expectations placed upon women and an ambivalence with womanhood. It resonated with me a lot; I grew up around a lot of very religious family members and had internalized a lot of those limiting expectations as a young person and only realized as an adult how harmful it had been for my mother to grow up surrounded by them and how harmful it was for me by proxy. As a family black sheep who is the daughter of a family black sheep, I was interested in writing a story about how people view the daughter as a reflection of the sins of the mother and the way the mother is treated trickling down to the daughter. There's layers of abstraction and fictionalization in this story—I'm only somewhat like Lina, her mother is almost nothing like my spirited, feisty mother, and my father isn't a demon (and in fact is very kind and supportive)—but the emotion behind it comes from a raw place.

About the Author

MATILDA LEWIS is a short fiction writer with a deep love of folklore, fairy tales and the Gothic. She lives in St. Louis, Missouri with her husband, a borderline-demonic tuxedo cat, and a slowly growing collection of animal bones. In her spare time, she enjoys dancing, painting, and playing the mandolin. Her media criticism can be found at *Blood Knife Magazine*.

Links

Twitter: @devilsdoorbell
Itch.io digital store: devilsdoorbell.itch.io

The Portrait of Venus

by Andrea Eberly

I made my first suicide pact with myself when I was sixteen, the year my mother could no longer tell me, *it's just in your head, you're such a lovely girl.* I was standing in front of a full-length mirror and my gaze traced the outline of my legs, sizing them up. My stomach filled with sharp stones.

When I can't wear skinny jeans. When people can tell. That's when I'll do it.

But even as my desperate feelings blossomed into that first concrete plan, I knew I was lying to myself, or at least exaggerating. I felt pretty good and liked being alive. Besides, I could still wear all sorts of shoes. Mules, flip flops, boots, slingback wedges, loafers, cha-cha heels. Size seven.

By senior year in high school, I had to stop wearing skinny pants and I started buying two different sized shoes.

The right side of my body is out of control. I am a monster.

How far away I feel from my symmetrical childhood when I used to sit on the couch with my mom and watch reruns of *In Search Of*. Leonard Nimoy narrated it, and the best episodes were the ones that explored places like the peaty soup of Loch Ness, deep and cold Lake Okanagan, and the dripping black vegetation of the Louisiana Bayou on the hunt for serpents and man-beasts.

I have a condition. It hit with puberty. Limbs are affected first, you see. Eventually tumors grow, mostly in the abdomen. Piles of plastic surgery handouts fill my drawers. I have spent hours reading about procedures like suction-assisted lipectomy, excision of excessive skin and subcutaneous tissue, and contouring or reducing facial bones. I am reminded of the Grimms' version of *Cinderella* in which the stepsisters cut their feet down to fit the golden slipper. Sometimes I wonder if they were really the villains of the story.

It was my third year of art school—I was wearing a size eight and a half—and I was flipping through an art book when I paused over an ivory figurine of a woman's head. I've never been hit by lightning (surely that would be a real piling on of random, unlikely events, and even I can't be that unlucky), but the way my fingers tingled, and my heart stopped in my chest, it was like I'd been struck by an arc of electricity.

She is one of the oldest representations of a human being that has ever been discovered. The Venus of Brassempouy.

Something may have gone terribly wrong with the fate of cells on the right side of my body, but I had a historical antecedent. She is kept at the Museé des Antiquités Nationales, Saint-Germaine-en-Laye, just outside of Paris.

And one side of her face is smaller than the other.

I graduated art school when I was still wearing a size eight and a half. That was around the same time I stopped wearing shoes that drew attention to themselves and settled on black leather Easy Spirits. I tried clogs and mules, which better accommodate a changing foot, but my gait is better in the sneakers. I always waited for Nordstrom's annual sale, which is in August, because I needed the discount. I started to hate August. Was it time to finally try on a size nine?

Bye-bye cha-cha heels.

Of course, it isn't just the shoes, but the rest of my covering is far less dramatic. I buy oversized (well, for half of me) pants and shirts. But wouldn't you know it with my breasts—they maintain an almost unnatural symmetry, so over the years I've only had to adjust the band-size.

Like a lot of artists, I make a living teaching. On my website, I've posted a single picture of myself. All the other photos are of my paintings in between lots of testimonials from parents who've hired me to give private art lessons to their kids. I'm sure the kids make fun of me from a safe distance, but one-on-one they're fine. Anyway, about that one photo—very up-close, my left side, the good side—it was taken with a Polaroid using black and white film. It is grainy the way only real film can be, and I think it is the only photo I like of myself. That includes the ones from when I was little, before I knew what hemihypertrophy was and that I had it. The left eye—my eye—is bright and clear and beautiful.

Hemi means *half*. Like hemisphere. And *trophy* means *growth*. Every idiot knows what *hyper* means. So half-hyper-growth.

Do the cells whisper to each other and dare the other one to split again, and again, and again? Press into my sciatic nerve. Shift my pelvis. Crunch my vertebrae and compress, compress, compress.

Muscle relaxants. Percocets. Oxycontin. Lidocaine patches. Antiepileptics and antidepressants and anything to convince those nerves to stop firing. I'm getting tired.

My preferred shoe brand only goes up to size twelves. I've decided that when I grow out of my size twelve extra-wide black sneaker, I'm going to make it all stop. I just won't stand to buy, and worse, have to *wear* a man's shoe. This is my line in the sand, my Alamo, and it sounds stupid, because it is, because everything sounds stupid if you really, really, think about it.

Anyway, the shoe thing has stuck. It is my ticking clock. A string of Augusts and sales and half-full shoeboxes. I hoped growing out of size twelves would not happen until my parents were already dead. I couldn't do that to Mom. Not to her. Mom always made it to opening night when I got a piece into a show unless she was out of town on business. She worked in insurance. Every week she invited me to Sunday dinner, and I almost never missed it.

Lucky me, Dad died of a stroke in his late fifties, and my right foot required a size ten at the funeral. And Mom got hit by a drunk driver the year I had to buy a size eleven. She was going to have retired in a month. The drunk driver hit her when she was on a business trip in Dubuque, Iowa. I never would have gone to Dubuque in my whole life except my brother was busy with his divorce and someone had to ID the body.

I'd never had much money, but with the death of my mother I knew I'd be splitting a sizable estate with my brother. I drained my savings for a first-class ticket and marked the passing hours of the flights from SeaTac to Chicago, Chicago to Dubuque with tiny bottles of Dewars.

The waiting room of the morgue was cool. I mean, the temperature was cool, like whoever designed it understood that grief robs a person of dignity anyway, so why add wet armpits to that? Too bad it didn't work. I was still really sweaty. The person talking to me said a lot of words and I nodded, and nodded, at how it can be shocking, at how she will be draped to hide the contusions, how how how—enough. I get it. Now, please, may I see her?

The room was small—like closet small—with beige-grey walls. There was a woman in the corner of the room. She wore a white coat over her scrubs, bright turquoise. For a moment I wondered if she was even real, or if she was some version of Mercury come to ferry my mother to another place. Or maybe she was there to keep me from doing something, like stealing the body and climbing to the top of a tower to lift the corpse over my head like a trophy and scream and scream and scream. Her necklace caught my attention. A silver-colored chain with an enameled Mickey Mouse face. I glanced at my mother, hesitating to touch or not to touch her and suddenly I was so pissed that I was even thinking about fucking Mickey Mouse at all. I'd rather think about *The Little Mermaid*, and not the stupid Disney version, but the original, the one my mother would read me before bed.

"Can you turn around for a moment?" I swallowed. "Please?"

Her lips puckered like she was considering my request, but rather than speak, she just turned toward the wall.

What an odd thing, seeing the body of my mother. What a strange thing to see a body that I had last seen a week before at Sunday dinner moving around her kitchen pulling out a hot lasagna and discussing a documentary on nickel mining in far northern Russia. Her eyes were closed—glued or something—but her mouth, her jaw. The bottom part of her face was completely sunken and purple. She must have hit the airbag pretty hard. I touched her hand. It was cold, firm. I already missed her skin.

That's not my mother. That's just her body.

I'm not my body.

My body is a monster.

What does Goodwill do with all the single shoes?

My chest felt so bruised from the agitation of my sad heart that I didn't work for two weeks. Maybe I would have stayed out longer, but I over-drafted my account and had to borrow from my brother. My students were happy when I came back. I guess they were worried that I was dying. We mostly worked in two dimensions but recently I've been pushing my painters toward sculpture so they can feel weight and know what it means to fill up space.

Now I have a tumor in my belly, at least I think it is a tumor. I don't know. I don't want to know. And it doesn't matter anyway because around the time it started to make my belly swell, I had just given in and ordered a pair of size eleven and half Easy Spirits. I couldn't wait till August. Anyway, the other day some lady with teased blonde hair and a teal windbreaker asked me if I knew if it was a boy or a girl. I was in the freezer aisle of the Gross Out—Grocery Outlet— deciding between Stoufer's lasagna and some cheaper brand I hadn't heard of. She had one of those WWJD friendship bracelets on her wrist. I told her it was twins—a boy *and* a girl and you should have seen that woman light up like I had just told her that Jesus was going to drop by for a cup of tea. I told her the father, my husband, was in Tanzania building a school with the church. I gave her one of the only phone numbers I knew by heart, the one for my favorite Indian restaurant and told her to call me so we could do bible study together. I didn't buy any lasagna and ordered Butter Masala with chicken instead.

Lake Tanganyika is in Tanzania and there is a monster living in it.

When the money from my parent's estate finally arrived, I paid my brother back, and then bought a plane ticket. I traveled overseas for the first time in my life. France. I had never forgotten about the Venus.

When I arrived at the museum, I found out the face was off display. The ivory was too delicate. The man at the front desk explained only people on a tour or part of the archeology community could see.

I cried. Not loudly. More like tears leaking out of my eyes and I told him my mother had just died, that I'd always wanted to see this relic, that I'd never had any money before and…

I held up my arm, motioned to my body.

I don't know how much longer I have left.

I don't know why they let their guard down around me. Maybe so many rules had already been bent letting me in without a tour, without a reservation, but the woman escorting me gave me a fine white glove that only fit on my small hand. I reached out and so gently brushed the face, the big side. She was so tiny, barely bigger than my thumb, the normal left one. Her face was triangular, and she had no mouth. Her head was covered in a hood of little squares. Or maybe they were supposed to be little braids. She was so finely wrought that it seemed impossible that the asymmetry of her face was an artifact of the natural flaws in the ivory. I knew it had to be my imagination; ivory doesn't conduct and even if it did my hand was wrapped in a silk glove, but it was like a shock when my finger brushed the big side of her face. I wanted to know who made this. I wanted to know the model, the artist's subject. Who was at the other end of this human chain, back before cars and electricity and mills and wheels and iron and bronze and fired clay? Back through the hips and wombs of women to a world without cities, writing, agriculture? Back to that day when this artist, this person who belonged to a world where people hunted to stay alive and knew the seasons of plants— back when humans still belonged to nature—sat with a piece of dead mammoth and a hard stone and captured this woman's image?

"It's beautiful, isn't it?" my escort asked.

"Very," I said, and nodded.

She told me everything she knew about the piece.

Would they have seen me as a goddess?

The day I ordered the size twelves, I went to Rite Aid and bought a vial of insulin. You can buy it over the counter, the regular insulin. I asked for a bag of syringes. The pharmacy tech glanced at my arm as he rang me up. At that moment, I decided to fill the oxycodone prescription I had been carrying around in my wallet. I really hoped when that tech went home that night, he told his girlfriend or boyfriend or whoever that some junkie was going home to crush up and inject some Oxys. Insulin, likely story. But they're getting very clever, these junkies. This one actually bought some insulin, too! Can you believe it?

Maybe I just imagined him looking at my arm, but probably not. It was twice the size of the other arm. The elbow had become a dark pit in the middle of peachy flesh and sometimes I would tell people I had been stung by a bee and that was why my arm was swollen because I was just so allergic. Disgust would turn to sympathy. Or maybe it was my imagination, and it was just another shade of disgust. And anyway, I know that tech wasn't just looking for track marks. I chewed an Oxy before I left the pharmacy because somewhere in my femur a colony of piranhas chewed up my bones from the inside.

The leg aches constantly from the pressure of all the extra lymph, and flesh, and whatever else makes up the rippling fat sausage-like thing that is what has become of my right leg. My leg is beautiful. My leg is a monster. The flesh bulges at the ankle and looks like it is melting over the tennis shoe. A size twelve. I used to have dainty feet and now I have only one dainty foot. I walk with a limp, I lean to the left.

For a while I considered wearing a chador with a veil. But I don't believe in God. It isn't about the promises we make but the ones we keep, and I can't wear pants. I can't walk. I can't make a fist with my right hand. I can't wear the shoes from the same pair. I can't order alcohol in a bar because I look pregnant. But I can buy it at the store and say it is for my husband who is coming back from Tanzania.

And I can inject a thousand units of insulin under my skin.

The threads holding together the side panels of my shoe split and my sock, a white athletic sock, yellowed with sweat, brown on the bottom because I don't clean and I don't wear shoes at home, peeks out and says hello.

Hello, your insulin will expire in three weeks.

I don't want to leave a mess. I take inventory of all the books I have, the piles stacked on the side of my bed, the ones next to the couch, the ones on top of the bookshelves. I don't want to look like a hoarder and a slob, but I don't want to give all the books away yet. When they come pick up my body, I don't want it to look like I wasn't cultured, that I didn't read. My gaze falls on my art books. Those will stay and maintain a prominent place on the shelf. They will say, "Oh, and she was an artist."

I flip through the old book and once again I see the Venus. I keep the page flipped to her and lurch and stump to the bedroom. I open the bedside nightstand (I've already thrown out the vibrators and dildos) and see the little cardboard box with the replica of the Venus I'd purchased at the museum in France. I remember the French-accented words of the woman who showed me the original.

The reason we say it is a portrait, and not just a sculpture or a representation or a figure, is because she has absolutely individual characteristics.

In *Cinderella*, the stepsisters hacked off parts of their feet to try to force them into the golden slipper. But there is no prince, no carriage, no castle, and I always liked *The Little Mermaid* better than *Cinderella* anyway.

I cut up chicken wire and lash it together with cables. I weave ribbons into it and smooth on newspaper strips dipped in a flour and water mixture. Trips to the art supply store on the Hill yield rubber cement and pigments and polyurethane. In my head the thing I picture is life-sized—my size—but soon I realize that it is turning out to be so very much bigger, filling the living room. Filling space. Unapologetically filling space. I keep thinking about that ivory head, about the hands that shaped it a thousand generations ago. How long would a parade of all those ancestors be? A mile? Why do we use the same words to talk about time and distance and location? I sculpt mismatched arms that melt into the torso and the mismatched legs erupt downward, both sides of the same thing. Deterioration. A disaster of rubble. What exquisite agony as I merge the plaster cast of my own face to the figure I crafted.

I always wondered: if the prince had known that it was like knives being driven into the little mermaid's soles every time she danced, would he have asked her to dance anyway?

My self-portrait, this amalgam of textures, colors, and pieces of my past, twisted and combined to maximally impact the observer, to reach out and grab their throat and heart. I twist wires to create a shoulder joint, a hip joint—she will be able to move—and smooth out the places where the parts meet. Memory and experience leave traces on a person. I've created a portrait of time, a record of the will for human contact. I have the right to take up space.

The little mermaid knew, the witch had told her, that when she traded her tail for legs that she would feel as though she was being cut in half very slowly and each step would create savage pain. Maybe the real question was this: would she have danced without a prince?

I turn on old jazz and the gravelly voice of the singer threads into me. My body wants to move.

I am not making a funeral pyre.

<hr>

Author's Note on "The Portrait of Venus"

While I was wandering around the Internet, I stumbled on an essay in which an art historian explained what makes a portrait special. This combined with an interest in exploring what it means to be inside of a body and my experiences working at a busy trauma center led to the initial written sketches that led to this story.

About the Author

Andrea Eberly's fiction has been published in such journals as *The Missouri Review*, *Witness*, and *Daily Science Fiction*. She lives in Seattle, Washington and works as a clinical pharmacist in critical care and emergency medicine. She is currently working on a novel.

Links
Author website: andrea-eberly.com
Twitter: @TheAndreaEberly

Gifted Speaker of the Silent Voice

by Samuel Marzioli

Patrick tightened his tie around his collar, watching his wife Reyna by the walk-in closet light. It warmed him to see her look so calm, all snuggled in her blankets. It reminded him of their early days some twenty years before, when happiness came cheap and good times weren't so few and far between. If only he had held onto that. If only she had too.

Ever since the move, she hadn't been the same. While she'd suffered from bouts of depression for as long as he had known her, it had only gotten worse within the last month. Even on her best days, she looked tired and perplexed, a somnambulist without the pretext of sleep. Add to that a difficult pregnancy and it was as if she were cruising down a dark road of potholes and black ice, with something large and threatening just beyond the high beams' lights. She refused to talk about it, and when he pushed her on the subject it only made things worse.

"Stop trying to fix me," she'd told him. "You can't talk my problems into non-existence. Doesn't work that way."

"I'm just trying to help," he said.

"If you want to help, then give me space and a little time to adjust, all right?"

At the memory, Patrick heaved a sigh and headed for the kitchen. After he poured himself his morning coffee in a thermos, he sauntered to the front door. As expected, a new dead thing lay upon the entryway rug, this time a cat curled up in repose, its meat and organs scraped away, bones scrubbed and polished to a pearl-like iridescence.

He had grown to accept Reyna's macabre obsessions— her dancing skeletons art prints, skull candles, even the taxidermy foxes flanking the stonework of the fireplace—because at least they *looked* like art. But these new animal "sculptures" pushed him well beyond his limits, made him think of sickness, rot, death. For the last four days, she had planted an assortment of them by the entrance: two squirrels caught in a fit of rage or passion, birds with the framework of their wings outstretched, a mother possum with the fragments of its babies still clinging to its back.

He couldn't bear the thought of touching it, so he fetched the broom nestled in the gap beside the fridge, threaded the shaft between the sculpture's ribs, hustled to the curbside trash, and flung it inside. Even this brief exposure had made his skin crawl, but the clatter of its drop brought a modicum of satisfaction. He would keep a few excuses primed to explain its disappearance, though Reyna hadn't said a word about the other ones, acted as if she hadn't noticed they were gone. Whether a good sign or a bad one, he didn't know and that frightened him the most.

Before he slid into his car, he glanced at his bedroom window and pictured Reyna still lying in their bed. He wondered what she'd do the moment he left. Start another sculpture? Hurt herself? Hurt their baby? Or maybe something worse?

He took a few deep breaths to ease his mind and calm the pressure in his chest, a tight pain flaring just behind his sternum. Heart attack or heartburn? Probably the latter since he hadn't yet keeled over—the key word being yet.

"I love you. Please be good," he said, a low whisper meant only for himself, and climbed into his car.

———•———

Patrick had left the closet open and now something inside it watched Reyna. She didn't think it was a peeping Tom and couldn't convince herself some intruder had crept in while she slept. No, this felt different, a presence entirely inhuman. Wedged somewhere behind the clothes and shoes and hangers, and swaddled in a blanket of dark, it stared at her with a naked need that said it wanted out.

Could it tell she wasn't sleeping? Did it know she could feel it watching, that peculiar mix of red-hot concentration saddled to a wave of cold? She hoped not. More importantly, she hoped never to find out. After throwing off her covers, she grabbed her glasses from the bedside table and bolted from the room, convulsing in the hallway as if to pitch off the heebie-jeebies squirming over her skin.

Even after soaking in a hot bath, she had no motivation, wanted only to collapse before the TV set. For months, the impending birth of Imogene had been paramount, but now more than ever she realized how important it would be for her to self-reflect. Patrick too, at least once he'd embraced the truth like she had.

Even as she thought this, she ducked into the nursery, its walls pink with purple trim, and a mural of a fluffy, white unicorn prancing up a rainbow arch. She had painted it. While far from photorealistic, it had a professional flair and she was proud of the results. Patrick, however, had bemoaned her gendered choice.

"Screw sugar and spice," he'd said. "And screw pink and soft and pretty. My baby will know no limits. 'Far as I'm concerned, she can be king."

Reyna hadn't disagreed. Still, until Imogene grew

old enough to make her own decisions, she didn't see the harm in making them herself. Mother knows best and all that. Besides, it was supposed to be fun, Reyna's reward for the baby's nine months of near parasitic dependence, and the ravaging effects it had on her body.

"Next time you push a baby from a small space between your thighs," she said, "you can decorate their room however you like."

"That's not fair."

"Fairness doesn't even factor. In the one-woman show called childbirth, I'm the cast, the crew, and the theater."

"If that's true," he laughed, "what does that make me?"

She shrugged. "You're the audience member who spilled his drink and got the theater floors sticky."

While that conversation had played out months ago, Reyna couldn't quite forget it and couldn't stop wishing she were back there, bundled in the joy of looking forward instead of this hopeless ache of looking back. Because something had gone wrong with the baby. Patrick called it her pessimistic nature and insisted geriatric pregnancies were always rough. But if so, why did she sometimes feel a strange sensation in her stomach? Pain and numbness, sure, but no less a tired weight gathering inside her as if something soft and mobile were growing hard and stiff. A pile of rocks, not life. Not anymore.

As she ambled through the nursery, she brushed

the crib rails, swiped a finger over the dresser, and stroked the texture of the mural's acrylic paint. She forced a smile and tried desperately to make it real. Within seconds, it slipped into a frown and only scratching at her arms seemed to drive the tears away.

"Doesn't matter what I know," she said, a whispered prayer to a god she hadn't spoken to in decades. "I want this. I need it. Please don't let anything take my baby from me."

A sudden shiver skittered down her spine from a feeling that she was no longer alone. As she fled the nursery, she tried not to notice the black gap between the wall and the closet's sliding door, ignored the feeling that something in that darkness watched her leave.

———————————————

When Reyna was an infant, her favorite toy was a baby doll. Its eyes were alight with wonder and its fat, pink cheeks creased with an overeager smile. Once she turned six, its small frame carved a nook into her arms and a dent into her pillow. How she cradled it, how she pushed it in her stroller, how she fed it from a bottle filled with water, never milk. She called it Imogene and would coo the syllables of its name into its ear.

"Im-mo-gene, you're so beautiful. Im-mo-gene, you're so sweet. Im-mo-gene, I love you."

She lost it on a drive across the country, when her

parents moved the family from the East Coast to the West. They were almost to their destination when she noticed, when she cried, "Where's Im-mo-gene? I can't find her!"

"Where did you see it last?" her father asked.

"I don't know."

"*When* did you see it last?" her mother asked.

"I don't know."

"Then how would we know where to look for it?"

"I don't know, but we have to go back. She needs me!"

Her parents didn't speak, couldn't risk sharing even knowing, furtive glances. While brute facts had already won them over, they knew no six-year-old would ever be convinced. They could have retraced every step, revisited every restaurant, shop, hotel, and rest stop in the nearly 3,000 miles of their journey and never found a trace, but Reyna wouldn't care. For Imogene, she would scour the world until the stars dropped from the firmament and the moon crashed into the sea.

Nevertheless, she was a child anchored to her parents' will. While they wouldn't let her spend a pointless minute searching, they couldn't stop her from sulking and crying. Endless days of wet, red eyes as the mournful oval of her mouth croaked Imogene's name. But she didn't give up. She'd seen movies where lost things trekked through perilous wildernesses or braved the rust and smog of countless overcrowded cities. No one ever expected to see them again, but there they were before the credits rolled, safe and snuggled in their owner's arms.

Reyna dreamed Imogene would do the same, that one morning she'd awake and find it resting by her side, pink cheeks still creasing with an overeager smile. It never happened. A loss like death soon settled over her, but for months she never failed to speak hope into the callous darkness of her bedtime.

"Im-mo-gene, I miss you. Im-mo-gene, I love you. Im-mo-gene, come back to me."

For hours, Reyna tried to concentrate on TV. She took in the sights and sounds of shows, but never any meaning. A big city girl since birth, living in the country overwhelmed her with all its quiet stillness and left her too long with her own morbid thoughts. Two months' worth of backwoods living and she was ready to call it quits.

Her fear of darkness didn't help. Even now, she eyed the shadows of the air vents, the space beside the fridge, the slit beneath the doorway to the basement in the kitchen's corner. Again, a feeling like she wasn't alone made her breath hitch and gulping air did nothing to relieve it.

She leaned across the couch's armrest and snatched the phone from its cradle. The car dealership had stringent rules about social calls that not even an

8-month pregnant wife could override. Still, if she could catch Patrick alone or on break, maybe he would answer. It rang three times before what she called the "Voice Mail Bitch" kicked in, and she slammed the phone down, then dropped back to the armrest with a sigh. Despite trying to affect a calm demeanor and even with a cool breeze pushing through the curtains behind her, she realized she felt warm. Maybe ill.

It was nothing like the sickness of her early months, with dizziness and migraines, and unpleasant confrontations with the contents of her stomach that she seldom won. This was something else, a suffocating pressure so familiar it triggered a sense of déjà vu.

She removed her glasses and pinched the skin between her eyebrows. At once, she imagined a favorite picture of her mother, black hair framing a round face and a piercing stare. She saw her East Coast family home, the columns of its patio, the red curtains and paneled windows that always reminded her of insect eyes. Then she heard her father, the low murmur of his bass voice spoken in her ear: "We call them the Mga Bisita."

Goose bumps flared across her arms and the chill within the living room increased. The Mga Bisita had been the bogeymen of Reyna's childhood. While some of her memories remained strong, the years had stripped away the rest of their vivacity and color, ghosts of recollections wandering the lost corridors of her mind. Nevertheless, she couldn't forget the feverish sensation that struck her whenever they were near.

Though slow in their approach—days instead of minutes—these sick bouts were happening again. But why? She had her suspicions but couldn't bear to parse them out quite yet. The idea overwhelmed her, sent the room spinning and put a tangled knot of worry in her chest. For the rest of the day, she slept and dreamed of bones, ancient gold, and something waiting in the shadows of her basement.

———

Patrick pulled up to the driveway about half past ten that evening. He rubbed his face, fingers pressing hard to work the tension from his forehead. Stock checks, paperwork, and sales plans still swirled inside his brain beneath the looming threat of unemployment.

"Guys, no one is getting fired," his boss Gary had said, during an afternoon meeting. "You're more than employees here; you're family."

Yet when Patrick had passed his office during lunch, he'd heard what sounded like "layoffs" used in cracking, whispered tones. It could have been "laughs" or "loaves, he supposed, but his boss's anguished look when they locked eyes belied such painless substitutions. Gary was an upright man. While Patrick didn't doubt his promise, even families had to cut the purse strings when times grew tough.

The moon appeared contemptuous, its rumpled face glaring down upon him as he traipsed the walkway to his house. He was about to head inside when he noticed something drawn onto the door, its color leaning orange in the porch lamp's jaundiced light. It appeared to be writing or a symbol of some kind. Thick, jagged lines formed its exterior with thin, wispy spirals for its center strokes. He swiped a finger through it. It was fresh, wet, and definitely blood.

"Reyna?"

His heart beat faster than his hands and feet could scramble as he jammed the key inside the lock. A ghastly image lurched into his mind of Reyna soaking in red water, and the deep-cut ruin of her wrists draped across the bathtub's rim. He almost screamed her name, almost lunged in the direction of the bathroom—but then Reyna sat up on the sofa, stretched her arms and yawned.

"You're home," she said.

Patrick took three steps and dropped onto his knees before her, rubbing her shoulders, her back, her sides, searching her body for any sign of a wound or bandage. He touched her stomach and rested his palms against her inner thighs. When he found nothing, he allowed himself a sigh.

"Ya gotta buy me dinner first, sailor," she said, her incredulous stare followed by a crooked smile.

"I love you," he said. "No matter what you do or say, I'll always love you."

"Okay." She shrugged. "Thanks? Work must have gone pretty well today to put you in such a friendly mood. Decent sales?"

"Not really. In fact, bad as usual. How was your day?"

Reyna shrugged. "Not great and I really don't want to talk about it."

He turned toward the entryway, thought about the sculptures, then directed his attention to the door and thought about the symbol there. One could gather blood in many ways and self-harm didn't have to be one of them. Slim comfort, but good enough for now. Just in case, he searched her expression for any sign of trouble, and finding nothing but the blankest stare, he slipped his arms around her legs and waist and hauled her in the air.

"Are you my Lyft?" she asked.

He felt the rumble of a silent laugh against his chest. "Yes ma'am! Where will it be?"

"I need you to take me to my bed, only…"

"What?"

"I lost my purse, and I don't have any money."

"Don't you worry, ma'am. I'm sure we'll figure out some way for you to repay me," he said, then winked, and carried her down the hallway to their bedroom.

───────────●────────────●───────────

Reyna's parents called it the Day of Bones, a ritual with the trappings of a celebration, dark magic mixed with a holiday's good cheer. Only Reyna and her parents knew about it because they had made it up. The day before, she and her father would decorate the house in white lace and black satin. Her mother would prepare a meal that was a Thanksgiving feast with some choice

Filipino dishes shuffled in. Turkey, cranberry sauce, corn and stuffing, but also lumpia, pandesal, and rice.

After they ate, they swapped presents by the fireplace: a collection of human bones, both in pieces or still whole. Whatever her father and mother could purchase from often less-than-reputable dealers from around the world. Disarticulated skeletons from China or India weren't uncommon, pieces doled out like chocolates from a candy box, each according to their preferences. Her father liked femurs for the weight and feel of them. Her mother liked humeri, which were far more manageable to a woman of such small stature. Reyna liked skulls—their haunting faces elegant as ivory—but she didn't complain, felt thankful for whatever part she ended up with.

In the early morning hours, a melancholy mood set in, like a funeral without tears. They set this time aside for silence and prayer. God was crucial for the occasion. Because when 3 A.M. rolled in, and a procession of slow clacks and rattles mounted up the basement stairs, followed by a hollow rap from behind the basement door, only the grace of God could keep the violence of the Mga Bisita at bay.

Her parents didn't allow her to trade directly; they told her she was much too young.

"One day," her mother said, "Your father will die, and his gift of understanding will pass to you, like it has for generations. Then you will see. Then you'll be able to speak with them yourself."

The moment they arrived, her mother ushered a sick and ashen Reyna up the stairs, forced her to wait the nervous minutes in her bedroom until someone came to fetch her out. She never caught a glimpse of these early-morning visitors, but she heard what passed for lungless voices and tongueless language. That rush of air, like steam passing through a kettle's spout before the boil made it sing.

Her parents did let her see the gold coins that followed, let her touch them, kiss them, throw them in the air and feel their satisfying weight fall around her. Roman solidi, Byzantine trachea, Spanish doubloons—all ancient, lost, forgotten treasures uncovered by this ancient, lost, forgotten tribe of men. Or near-men. Or not-men. Or post-men. Her parents didn't know and the Mga Bisita had never bothered to explain it.

———•———

Another day passed in a fit of boredom, unease, and nausea, though Reyna slept away the majority of it. As soon as the sun went down and the grass of the surrounding acres settled to a sea of black with fireflies hovering like a galaxy of stars above it, she awoke with a start. She had the vague impression of hearing noise muted by the walls or distance. Had the sound been the vestige of a dream? Or had Patrick come home?

Relief took her gently by the hand and she almost danced with it in rapture. Of course it was her husband.

He often spent long hours at the job and came back about this time of night. When it came to selling cars, one didn't simply pitch numbers at passersby, hoping one would stick. It took time, effort, and often a stroke of luck. Sadly, these days luck was in high demand and short supply, and her husband's shifts grew longer.

"Patrick?" she called out. Breath like incense smoke spilled from her lips and she drew her arms across her chest for warmth. "Why didn't you wake me?"

No response. She heard a thump and then a creak that might have been the hinges of a door. From where, she couldn't gather, and yet her thoughts rounded on the master bedroom's closet, and how—after her last experience with the presence inside—she'd made a point to keep it shut. She imagined Patrick changing from his suit into pajamas, his eyes half buried in the puffy, purple lids beneath them. He was tired, or couldn't hear her, that's all.

"Patrick… answer me," she said. Emphatic at first, but when the silence lingered, her voice softened, and her plea was muffled by the tightening of her throat.

Another set of thumps and creaks, a slow progression growing closer, louder until it clarified into footsteps and the groaning of old wood. But it wasn't coming from the master bedroom or its closet; it was creeping up the staircase beyond the basement door.

Reyna had expected this for days now, but she wasn't ready for it yet. She shivered, tried to stand, but collapsed back onto the sofa. Her legs had fallen asleep and refused to support her. The more she forced them, the more her numb discomfort transformed into an electric ache. She was nowhere near able to drag herself to safety by the strength of her arms alone, so she sat, and watched, and listened.

The footsteps stopped beyond the walls of the kitchen. The basement doorknob shifted with a metallic sound of stretching springs and grinding metal. She closed her eyes, a helpless last resort, and the world exploded in a flurry of sound all but drowned out by her screaming.

"Someone help me! They're coming for my baby!"

An enduring moan. A crash. A guttural shout, and heavy stomps made the floorboards vibrate as they converged on her position. Hands seized her by the shoulders. She lashed out, slapping and scratching at every inch within her reach before a familiar voice wrenched her from the grip of her confusion.

"Reyna! Reyna, it's me!"

She opened her eyes to find Patrick, teeth gritted, his face half mad with worry.

"Are you alright?" he asked. "What happened?"

She shook her head so hard it hurt. As fast as her now half-numb legs allowed, she climbed onto her feet and stumbled into his embrace. Cool air rushed through the open front door and soothed her panicked warmth. Any sense of relief vanished when she turned in the direction of the basement. Its entrance yawned wide and from the closest edge, stark, white fingers uncurled from the door frame and receded back into the darkness down below.

•————————————•

Patrick stared up at the ceiling, his body stiff and straight with Reyna tucked into the crook between his chest and arm. The way her eyebrows arched, and her mouth formed a perfect "O," she looked serene—a choir boy belting out a silent note—and he didn't want to wake her. After everything she'd been through, it was the least he could do.

The Sack Time Inn seemed to have the opposite intent. An ice machine's vibrations rocked the outer wall, its rolling hum broken only by the "chug" of new ice sliding into the old. Somewhere in the distance, car doors slammed, a dog barked, followed by a child's happy chatter. If he held his breath and perked an ear, he could even hear the snores from the occupants next door, punctuated by someone's high pitched, nose-like whistle.

"Our baby isn't safe." That was the first clear thing Reyna had said after he had found her. The rest of her story had been a jumble of words tripping over words and flattened by a nervous stutter. Dead men, bones, and basements. He couldn't make sense of it, or didn't want to, and she didn't wait for him to work it out. She had merely grabbed him by the arm and dragged him to the car.

He'd dutifully obeyed when she had insisted they stay somewhere else that night. Never mind the cost. Goodbye gas or food next week. Despite his obvious concern and accommodations, she had still gone to sleep angry. It was his fault, he knew—the way he excavated answers with a pickax tone—but he couldn't let the subject drop no matter how much she begged him.

"I told you already. If you didn't believe me before, why would you believe me now?" she'd asked him when he had pressed her. Then "It was my imagination." Then "Nightmares, okay?" when he'd pressed her even harder.

Not that he had been any more forthcoming. He didn't tell her about the thing he had seen when he came home that night, how he'd reached the porch stoop when something unexpected caught his eye.

A figure had peered at him, crouching by the downspout beyond the house's far off corner. With the porch lamp off, and the stars and moon obscured by clouds, Patrick could distinguish nothing but its basic form. Human at a glance, but misshapen: an oversized head perched upon a shriveled frame, and limbs stretched so long and thin they might have been branches.

It had gestured at him, or so he thought, the way what might have been its hand raised, and what might have been its finger snapped erect. He'd heard an exhale broken by a rise and fall in tone that seemed to aim at words but missed.

"Who's there?" he'd asked.

The figure ducked behind the corner, merging with the shadows of the house. Once he triggered the flashlight on his phone, he'd followed, searching the side yard, the backyard, and the distant field where grass absorbed the sound of everything but wind and chirring crickets.

When Reyna screamed, he'd turned back home. All thought of the figure vanished, but in the relative quiet of the motel room his mind refused to let it go. It could have been one of the dead men Reyna spoke of. Then again, blurred movement in the woods could have been Bigfoot, a light streaking through the sky could have been a UFO, and the sauce stain on his tie last week could have been the leavings of the Flying Spaghetti Monster.

Based on the speed at which the figure had moved, and the beastly noise it had made, it was probably an animal. Nevertheless, he kept it to himself. Reyna's mental state had flagged enough without the added stress of some unknown beast skulking around their property.

Eventually, he allowed himself to sleep and had a series of disconcerting dreams. In them, the figure crouched in the master closet, slowly pressing on the door until it slipped into their room. Patrick would wake the moment its front paws planted on the bedside, its hot, raw breath blanketed his face, and the daggers of its teeth descended. Once he fell asleep again, the scene repeated, the substance of a fever dream without the fever.

Sometime in the dark of early morning, he groped for Reyna's hand, fumbling through layers of empty sheets and the crevice of her pillow. He scanned the room. Reyna now stood by the far wall, her skin cadaverous in the smoke alarm's green light. He almost called her back to bed when he heard her say, "How did you find us?"

It took a moment before Patrick realized she was facing the communicating door. The door was open, and something moved within the darkness brimming on the other side. A sound like leaking air—a hiss?—and Reyna said, "How can I trust you after everything you've done?" Another rush of air—a breath?—and then, "I know. I've known it for some time now. Yes, I understand, but…" she gestured toward Patrick, "I don't think he ever will."

Patrick shivered, and only clenching his jaw kept his teeth from chattering. He couldn't stand to watch the way she moved—her rigid, violent shaking—so he turned away and pretended to be asleep. By the time she crawled back into bed and draped an arm across him, he didn't have the nerve to speak.

He could only imagine her lost within the field beyond their house, looming over something dead, its ribs spread like the crimson petals of a flower and the glasses perched above her grin reflecting blood-stained hands. If not for the distraction of a sweat bead sliding down his face, he might have shuddered.

Reyna turned thirteen the day before her parents sat her on the couch and filled the much-too-narrow space beside her. They gave no explanation and the only clue she had to go on was their nervous energy that made them break their oh-so-stern expressions with fits of giggles.

"We're going to have a baby!" they said, a synchronized cry they had obviously practiced.

"Oh," said Reyna. It wasn't so much news as confirmation what with the way her mother floated through the house, her smiles beatific, a warm, red glow effusing from her cheeks. "Congratulations, I guess."

For days after, the promise of a younger sister or brother weighed heavy on her soul. Friend or enemy? Sibling or slave? She didn't know what to think and not just because it meant extra noise, distractions, and babysitting gigs that paid in little more than thank yous. She still remembered the lesson she had learned when Imogene went missing: nothing good ever lasts. Whether or not she had the right to feel that way, there it was, a dime-sized tumor that had been lodged inside her brain since childhood.

The Day of Bones neared as eight months swelled heavy beneath her mother's blouses. With the profits, her parents had their sights set on a nicer crib, not that dusty, creaking heap of Reyna's, still stuffed up in the attic. Once they ate their feast, said their prayers, and the mantel clock chimed its 3 A.M. alarm, the Mga Bisita came.

Reyna retreated to her room, but she always imagined the events that followed as if she'd stayed. As soon as they entered, the Mga Bisita motioned to her mother, touched her stomach, fondled it. Her mother ran and her father, angry beyond words, had shouted until the Mga Bisita retreated to the darkness, back the way they came.

The baby died soon after. They named him Antonio. Committed to God in prayer and baptized by his family's tears, they interred him in a coffin much too small to fill its cemetery plot. As they stood before the gravesite after the ceremony ended, her father gnashed his teeth and her mother wailed. Reyna cried as well, though quietly and to herself. A worn-out sort of mourning, like an addendum to a sadness that had started long ago.

Reyna's mother insisted Antonio's death had nothing to do with the Mga Bisita, but Reyna had to wonder. After all, they had begged for him. Now that he was nothing more than spoiled meat sloughing off of brand-new bones, they'd gotten exactly what they wanted.

———•———

Reyna forgot to wear her glasses. As she sat, back pressed against the motel's outer wall, the bleary view of streets and strip malls didn't concern her because her tears would only blur them anyway. As soon as Patrick left, she wouldn't have the strength to hold them back. She took a sip of coffee, placed a hand upon her belly, imagining the prize beneath the inches there.

"I know you're trying. I know you're fighting for your life, and you need to keep your strength up, but please show Mommy you're still there."

She didn't need it to be real; only timing mattered. Her organs could shift, her uterus expand, or gas could bully through her bowels, provided it felt right. All she wanted was a reason to hold on, not this twinge of dead weight, this dagger through her heart and stomach.

Imogene hadn't kicked in twenty-seven days. It wasn't a guess. Reyna had started counting when she felt the first stabbing in her gut, and the quick trip to the ER that left her and Patrick reeling. Hours of pacing, hugging, crying. When the doctor returned with the test results, they held their breath, preparing for a shock, all but planning for a funeral. However, the news was good. The baby looked well, and with no dilation the pain that Reyna felt must have been a cramp.

"Go home," the doctor said. "Drink two big glasses of water and get some much-needed rest. Everything will be fine."

Except it wasn't fine. Reyna realized it sooner than the morning after. A conversation with Aunt Alma, her mother's sister, only proved the point. The women in their family never had much luck with childbirth. They weren't barren, but maybe something worse: like a grove where the trees tended to grow slanted, or a garden where the plants bore hollow fruit. Her parents had conceived four times, but Reyna, their third child, was the only one who'd lived.

Patrick never listened to her warnings. He put more stock in doctors and hard science than hearsay and a mother's intuition. If she had to pick one thing to explain the strain between them, it was this far more than his long hours at work. She let him keep his faith, and in the meantime, she held onto the fragments of her own, waiting for some future time when facts could prove her wrong. Too bad they hadn't.

The front door squeaked, and she turned to find Patrick dressed for work.

"How are you feeling?" he asked. "Are you going to be okay by yourself?"

"I'll be all right," she said, her throat so dry she almost croaked her answer. "If I need anything, I'll call."

Patrick nodded. He pressed his lips against her cheek, a kiss devoid of passion, the affection of distant cousins who had only just met. It hurt her, but she embraced it. She didn't need his love right now, only his understanding. Or if things turned out the way she knew they would, possibly his forgiveness too.

She waited until Patrick's car pulled out and the dust clouds of the gravel lot whisked him to the road before she stepped inside the murk of their room. Since she had seen firsthand the shape of things that lived in darkness, darkness didn't have the same effect. She now knew the Mga Bisita watched her, and that certainty replaced her fear with a self-conscious apprehension. It made her clumsy, as if she'd grown new arms and legs, and her brain hadn't mastered the rhythm of their movements yet.

She headed straight for the communicating door, placed a palm against the wood. She imagined a Bisita standing on the other side, its carpals bent before the distal phalanges started rapping, and its mandible parted from its maxilla as air spewed from its mouth. The thought tickled her in a way she didn't like. She laughed, desert dry and void of joy, and took another sip of coffee.

Numbness kept the tears away, so she stared dry-eyed at the blur of the bathroom's wall until the texture of the paint began to drift, and the hate she felt for God and life and happy, smiling parents sizzled like a ball of fire within her. Because she hadn't felt a kick in twenty-seven days, and regardless of how the night progressed, she never would again.

———————

By early evening, Patrick stepped into his cubicle to unpack his lunch. He didn't have an appetite, but he'd been on his feet all day— pacing the empty, sun-baked lot— with only sweat and memories for company. He'd earned the right to a lunch break, and hell if he wasn't going to take it.

As he peeled the wrappings, he stared at the image of him and Reyna on his desk, the pair of them high up on a mountain bridge. With hands clasped, they leaned back against railings made of ropes, the crisp green of treetops down below, and the effervescent white of clouds above them. Picturesque and perfect, the kind of photo they might have put in the frame before he bought it.

He loved that picture. Not just the thought of something good, but the trust entailed, a trust he couldn't find inside himself right now. For that Reyna, he had risked a lethal drop because he knew she would never fail to be his balance. As for the other Reyna, the one waiting for his return? He'd never felt afraid of anyone before, but he feared her—both for what she'd done and what she had become.

What was one supposed to do when their lover went insane? Ride the wave, or wait and let it crash and drown you? For a while, he had done the latter and called it hope, but maybe that had always been wishful thinking. Or cowardice.

Deep down, he realized that if any of his foundations were removed, the edifice would crumble, and the meaning of his life would slip away. He didn't have the strength to deal with that, not now, maybe not ever.

He heard a muffled knock and turned to find Gary knuckling the cubicle partition, his usual grin replaced by a decisive frown. His heart jumped, a deep throbbing in the center of his chest at why his boss had come, and what he knew it meant.

"Patrick," Gary said. "We need to talk."

When Reyna turned seventeen, she was ready to see a world outside the limits of her parents' home. That meant distant schools and dorm rooms, and a car good enough, at least, to putter. By the end of senior year, she had been accepted by several colleges: her choice of coasts and a few scattered in between. All she needed were the funds to make it happen.

"I think it's time we planned for your future," her father said at dinner. "The Day of Bones isn't for months now, but when it comes, we'll trade for you."

Reyna didn't understand and turned to her mother.

"What he's trying to say is we've squirreled enough away to keep us safe and comfortable for some time," her mother said. "That means whatever school you choose, that's where we'll send you."

"Are you sure?" asked Reyna. "I don't know what to say!"

"We'll take 'Thank you,'" said her father.

"And hugs and kisses too."

For the remainder of their meal, they shared food and laughter, sparking memories of good times old and new. Reyna had never felt so elated. She retired to her room that night, mind racing with countless possibilities that had, until now, always seemed phantasmal. After jacking headphones into her desktop, she browsed pictures of campuses, brainstormed majors, checked weather patterns, and researched bookstores and coffee shops based in the cities of her favorite schools. She was so absorbed, she barely heard the frantic thudding up the stairs, or the violent drumming on her bedroom door that followed.

Her mother charged inside, sobbing, breathless, her face and clothes soaked in more than sweat and tears. Reyna never forgot her mother's expression that night, how it had shifted between a grimace and a grin, as if terror and insanity battled for the right to shape her face.

"Mom, what's wrong?"

Her mother didn't say a word, simply pressed a palm against her chest and left the room. Reyna scurried after her, slowing her pace when she caught up to her mother on the stairs. They took the final steps together, then her mother clenched her hands to fists and gestured. Reyna's father lay upon the entry tile, his body deflated, skin sunk over the knotted remnants of his insides—a fabricated thing, a cheap rubber likeness of the man he used to be.

It took days before her mother had the strength to tell her what had happened, how the Mga Bisita had surprised them when they stormed into the house. They motioned at her father and encircled him, whispered secrets in his ear. While her father didn't seem concerned at first, his face soon paled with dread.

He babbled as he turned a sagging grimace toward Reyna's mother, his pleading eyes shedding all their light. One of the Mga Bisita kneeled beside him as he sank onto the floor. Fingers slim as needles twiddled at his sides, unknitting skin and muscle and loosening the flesh until his skeleton slid free.

Within minutes, what was once a husband and father twitched, scarlet-stained collagen and calcium imbued with life. The body shivered, limbs thrashing in a drowning man's helpless panic, before the jaw spread in something like a silent scream.

The Mga Bisita helped it to its feet and then formed a line before it. It followed their procession with a careful, child's plodding down the basement stairs, still gawking at the sight of what had once been its home. The light and shadows shifted in its orbits when it glanced at Reyna's mother. She almost thought it recognized her face as it stepped farther into the darkness and disappeared from sight.

———

Reyna paced the slim walkway outside her motel room and watched the sun set, its fires reduced to embers beneath a filter of clouds. When the light faded to a smeared blush, she headed back inside and laid a few black t-shirts and white paper napkins across the surface of tables and countertops, and the arms and seats of chairs. She didn't mean it to be silly; it was supposed to be a tribute to her childhood, the way she and her father used to decorate the house. Once night fell, she doubted she would care, but it seemed significant right then—the merging of her past and present—even if she couldn't define the reasons why.

After she changed from pajamas to a loose, blue cotton dress, she dragged an armchair closer to the window. A shy assemblage of clouds had slung their bellies closer, and now the sky hung black in judgment, as if the moon and stars were embarrassing creations that God had scribbled out. Her neighbors' loud disregard continued from last night, but this time it felt different, muted by her expectations and a keen awareness of the shadows gathering behind her. The wind blowing through the screen felt warm, more like breath than air. Yet something inside it chilled her all the same, making the thin, transparent hairs across her arms stand on end.

She finished a light Chinese takeout dinner in honor of her mother's feasts, then closed and locked the window and drew the curtains tight. If she was going to make it through the night, she needed time to rest, to calm her mind and blunt the savage spikes in her emotions.

She had only taken a step when a knock resounded from the communicating door. Her breath hitched in her throat and the pressure in the room magnified a hundred-fold. When she'd agreed to the Bisita's proposition, it promised they would come at nightfall, but she had no idea it meant the very hour.

She shut her eyes and pictured Imogene, no bigger than an eggplant, asleep within the peaceful dark inside her. The tears she cried felt all too familiar. They were not just a continuation of some older grief, but the kind that had endured too long and had finally reached a proper end.

It took minutes for her eyes to adjust to the dull light leaking through the curtain edges. Longer before she had the strength to stand, to move her stiff, unwilling legs. Longer still before she forced herself to throw the communicating door open.

The Mga Bisita entered one by one and then fanned out along the perimeter of the room. Four more crept in later, one taller than the others and three smaller than the rest. None of them looked anything like she'd imagined. With their affinity for bones, she'd pictured them dressed like death in black, hooded robes rippling like liquid shadow. Instead, they wore strips of leather the pink and tan of human skin, which covered everything but their orbits and their fleshless grins. They looked more like hunters obscured beneath ghillie suits than grim reapers, but they were no less foreboding.

Reyna turned to face the tallest Bisita.

"Dad?" she said.

The word soured on her tongue, and she regretted it at once. While the Bisita had told her of its past, the skein of flesh it wore, the memories created when it called itself her father, it was no longer him. It wasn't even human and no amount of reminiscing over old, decaying bones would change that. It had a new identity, a new wife, new sons, and now it wanted a new daughter. Her daughter. Her baby, Imogene. To peel her skin off, and untangle muscles, organs and veins until only glistening white remained.

It stared down at her, released air from the cracks between its teeth. It was a violent sound, a bestial decree, but when the meaning of the noise occurred to her, she knew it meant her no harm.

An ache filled her up to bursting; the choice had come at last. Should she let Imogene live a few more weeks so she could die a natural death, or should she let the Mga Bisita have her daughter so Imogene could thrive and grow as only their kind could?

Neither option gave Reyna joy, but she knew which one she wanted, knew that life had prepared her for this moment from the very start. She glanced down, placed her hand against her belly to memorize the look, the feel, the fullness. One last mental snapshot for the dark times up ahead, for when withdrawals from her love for Imogene truly started.

"What do you need me to do?"

———•———

Patrick finished work by 7, tossed his things into a little box, and was on the road by 7:15. It felt strange to see other drivers filling up the city streets leading to the highway and not the easy, breezy cruising he was used to. Nowhere near the choke of proper gridlocks, but still moving at a plod. He once referred to this as "a thin cough of traffic," a phrase applied to any car queue less than congestion. Blame it on fatigue, but it had made him chuckle. If only he could think up another silly phrase to take the edge off, but he didn't have the capacity for wit or laughter.

Occupied by thoughts of home, he almost missed his motel turn, was forced to take a sharp left, rubber skirting the edges of the pebbled shoulder. His things tipped and clattered as the box slid the length of his backseat, a sound like the slow enunciation of his failure. Getting fired was hardly a surprise; he'd long expected it. Still, to actually hear the words, to live and breathe the repercussions? It hurt his heart as much as his pride.

Shortly after Gary had stepped into the cubicle, he'd dropped a hand on Patrick's shoulder and spoke into his ear.

"I'm afraid we're going to have to let you go. I know what I promised, but things are worse than I let on. If I don't make drastic changes soon, I risk losing everything."

Patrick had put on a brave face and rambled off some line about understanding. They shook hands. Once he'd collected his things, reality began to warp, stretching seconds into minutes, every foot of carpet swelling into miles. He took the sympathy and well-wishes from his co-workers with smiles and nods, but by the time he had reached his car, he broke. He had left that place a smaller man, sunken in the fabric of his suit.

Only the gravel popping and grinding beneath his wheels snapped his introspective daze. He pulled into an empty spot closest to his motel room, cut the engine, and then gripped the steering wheel with his gaze fixed upon the windshield's dirt and smudges. How was he supposed to tell Reyna? Could she handle such a drastic change so soon after the last one? All things considered, could *he*?

He might have sulked for hours had he not noticed the blood splotch on his motel door, a drip of red sinking like a backslash through the numbers. He imagined Reyna lying prostrate on the bathroom floor, shards of glass lodged into her arms and neck and scattered all around her.

Not again, he thought as he hustled to the door and slammed his keycard in.

The reader beeped and the door flew wide, but the sight of men filling up the room, and Reyna—dress hiked up around her waist—stopped him short of entering. His mind was a colony of ants suddenly exposed, his thoughts the panic and confusion of the scrabbling workers. Whether he'd discovered Reyna cheating or being raped, it made no difference to the madness that controlled him.

Pain erupted. The muscles in his chest tightened, squeezing the inferno blazing in the space behind them, ripping rivulets of sweat from his pores. Once the fire spread into his arm, he hunched to catch his balance.

"Reyna?"

The men standing closest dragged him in and slammed the door. Blinded by the dark, overpowered by the presence of untold strangers, all Patrick could do was sink his nails into his ribs and slump onto the floor. He heard Reyna's squealing, screaming repetition of his name. It seemed to come from some far-off place, like a haunted memory.

All he wanted was to hold her hand, to rest his head against her lap, to feel her kiss, and he wondered why she hadn't come to him by now. He would have called to her again, but his gasping breaths no longer brought him air. The strangers encircled him and the almost plastic touch of hands stripping off his clothes, pressing hard against his naked skin, made him forget his need to have her close.

After twenty years of marriage, he never thought it would end this way, with so much left to mend and so much left unsaid. He stretched his hand toward Reyna, pictured her alone with Imogene. Would they be happy when he was gone, or lost without him? He didn't know the answer and regret made his feeble body shudder.

I'm sorry, he thought just before the darkness and the cold sank into his pores, invaded him, and he fell into the void's embrace.

●━━━━━●

They gave Reyna's mother six months to live, but she only lasted half that time before her sickness took her. By then, her destruction was complete: a broken heart, a broken soul, and with her skin like parchment wrapped around cancer-hollowed bones, a broken body too. She didn't wake up once in the days before her death. Reyna took it as a kindness since consciousness only brought her mother pain. Still, it meant no last hugs, no final conversation, no definitive goodbye. Just her stale warmth and struggling breath as Reyna waited by her bedside.

Reyna had asked the Mga Bisita to come. Months of standing by the basement door, pleading to the darkness down below, thinking every creak may have been an answer. To see her mother rise up from her broken shell would have brought her so much comfort, and besides, it seemed fitting that a woman who traded in bones would live on as bones on the far side of eternity. But what was fitting didn't matter in the grand scheme of things and the dead men never came.

After they interred her mother between her father and brother's cemetery plots, Patrick drove her home. As they lay in bed together, Reyna cradled in Patrick's arms, he said, "I wrote a poem after my grandfather passed. It was about how our sadness is a chain connecting us to those who died, and how the only way to set them free is to learn to live without them. I know it doesn't help much, but I always thought it was a nice idea."

Reyna bit her lip, just enough to suppress her anger. Patrick always floundered in the presence of her grief. Since her mother's death, not a day went by where he didn't offer up some quote or precious memory, as if her emotions were debris that some clever words could sweep away.

"I wish that were true," she said in a careful, measured tone. She pressed the cup of her ear down, sealing the edges with his skin, taking in the reassuring rhythm of his heartbeat. This. This sound was all she needed, not the sloppy content of some bereavement card. "But I don't think the dead care much about anything anymore."

She felt him jerk, what might have been a shrug.

"I can't remember the last time I had two bits of faith to rub together, but if there is something after death, maybe it doesn't matter what we believe. Who knows? What's coming might surprise us both."

The thought of Patrick lying in a coffin struck her hard, and she leaned back to peer into his face. "Please don't die. I love you too much to lose you, too."

His sad eyes, his lopsided grin, and the rumble of his chuckle filled her ear. "I wish I could promise that."

"You can. Just say, 'I promise!'"

"Reyna…"

"Fine, then how about this? No matter where you go, or how long it takes for me to follow, promise that you'll wait for me on the other side."

He squeezed her once, pulled her closer. "Okay. I promise."

Imogene was born still, but not stillborn. She had no light inside her eyes, only closed lids swimming in a pool of shadows, her pale cheeks much too stiff to crease. Reyna only held her for a moment—the pillow heft of such a tiny thing—but it felt so much like a dream come true. The doll she'd lost, that she had idolized across a span of decades, had returned as something better than the plastic thing she'd prayed for.

"My Imogene. You're so beautiful. You're so sweet and I love you very much," she said before the Mga Bisita took her.

Reyna couldn't watch as her once-father performed the rite of transformation. If the thought of Imogene being opened and dismantled broke Reyna's heart, the sight of it would have destroyed her. She waited until she heard something like a kitten's feeble purr and turned in time to catch a glimpse of tiny bones struggling in her once-father's arms. After that, she laughed and cried as the Mga Bisita raised their silent voices in a hum of celebration.

Only an electric beep stopped them short. The latch bolt clicked and the door swung wide. Daylight spewed into the muddled dark, eclipsed by a figure filling up the doorway.

"Patrick?" Reyna shifted to her side, squinting through the harsh blur of light. "Patrick, why are you back so early?"

Patrick lurched and gurgled, his movements stilted before he froze in place. "Reyna?"

Two Mga Bisita dragged Patrick in and forced the door closed. Patrick collapsed onto the floor, his breaths whooping loud and heavy as he clutched his chest.

"Patrick," she said, her voice straining for a shout she couldn't muster. "Patrick?" She tried to climb onto her feet, but Imogene's birth had drained her of her strength and she managed only to tilt her head and wobble. "Patrick, what's wrong with you? Please answer me!"

He didn't, or couldn't. His breathing began to stall, to soften, and his burdened writhing slowed—a wind-up toy inching toward its final motion. If only she had bothered to explain when she had had the chance, not just recite what a lifetime of experience had convinced her of, but make him listen until he finally understood. She couldn't have predicted the shock of finding her like this would kill him and yet she couldn't help but blame herself. With one hand, she'd made her oldest dream come true and with her other she'd brought forth her greatest nightmare.

"Help him," Reyna said to the Mga Bisita.

They didn't move. Their empty orbits fixed on her, passive grins displaying nothing but disinterest.

"Change him. Make him one of you, or so help me God, I'll never trade with you again. No more bones." She took a haggard breath. "And no more babies."

Reyna's once-father gestured and the Mga Bisita began a reluctant march to Patrick's side. They crouched beside him, obscuring him behind a curtain of their shredded leather. The squish of tender organs shifting and all the while Reyna closed her eyes and chanted "Patrick": one last stab of desperate hope filtered through that single name.

———————————

He released his pain, not as the raucous scream he intended, but as a long and airy breath. His body thrashed against his will, but those beside him held him down until he spent the greater portion of his panic. Once calm, the details of the room poured into his eyes as if the barrier inherent in the darkness had been stripped away, revealing structures, textures, substances, dimensions—things presented in and by themselves, without reference to their shade or color. It gave him a new appreciation of his surroundings. Only a cheap motel of fiberboard and dust, but with his new sight, it had all the splendor of a palace.

He sat up.

"Patrick, Patrick, Patrick," Reyna chanted, eyes closed, her body scrunched into a ball amid a stain of blood and amniotic fluids.

His brothers helped him to his feet by the handles of his ribs, a hum spilling from their mouths in silent welcome. They formed a line. What was once Patrick watched as his new father led the procession, followed by his brothers, and then his mother—still cradling his once-daughter, who panted out the gibberish of her age.

Before he followed, he glanced at Reyna and a

pang of longing filled the hollow of his chest. The sensation was more a memory of ache, a phantom pain, than something real. He almost passed her, but she crawled across the bed and caught his arm.

"Patrick, wait!"

He hesitated, parsing out the syllables of her words as they played against his new ears. He knew the meaning, of course. While he had changed, he was still the person he had always been, with all the same experiences and memories. But "Patrick" no longer held the same meaning; it was a name for flesh alone. He meant to shrug her off, to follow the silent siren's song flowing through the portal, calling him to his new home, when Reyna shouted, "You promised me!"

He grabbed her by the wrists, rubbed them with his phalanxes, feeling for the bones beneath. Such delicate symmetry. Such fine articulation. He'd never thought of her as strong, but now he saw her strength was magma spilling through her hidden chambers. He wanted her, that beauty, that vigor, hiding behind a lie of flesh, but he could not take it now. The darkness whispered secrets directly to his mind, knowledge meant only for his kind, and there were rules about Gifted Speakers such as her that he must never break. With bones that cracked and snapped, but never healed, he would need her alive for as long as she was able.

As for the promise? With his new sight, he could observe the clockwork of her body counting down the remainder of her life. When years faded into days, he would find her and leave his gifts around her home. He would paint his mark upon her door to stake his claim. Then he'd watch and wait. When her remaining hours withered into minutes, he would come to strip the stain of life from off her bones and make her into a new creation. Wife if she still wanted, or daughter if she didn't.

He leaned in close and with his new voice breathed a renewal of his promise into her face. It surprised him how hard it was to let her go, to separate from her touch, but he did, because he had to. This world of beating hearts and soft, decaying flesh was the memory of a prison and he didn't want it anymore. He motioned to the gold his brothers had left behind; a great, round sack of untold riches. It would mean nothing to her now, but when she healed, she would know its worth.

One last look at Reyna, his once-wife and now Gifted Speaker of the Silent Voice, before the pull proved too great. His new home—cities made of bones and stitched flesh, mounds of skulls piled high as mountains, rivers flowing thick and red with blood—called to him. He stepped through the communicating door and through the portal beyond, following his new kin into the majesty of endless dark and the harmony of everlasting silence.

●━━━━━●

AUTHOR'S NOTE ON "GIFTED SPEAKER OF THE SILENT VOICE"

This story began as an image in my head of a man proffering human bones to a pair of living skeletons. I wanted to explore the themes of misunderstanding and perspective, particularly how one's worldview can shape the same set of events into contradictory interpretations. Neither Reyna nor Patrick knows what truly happened in the past or present, but by the end there's enough information for the reader to discover what both of them are missing.

ABOUT THE AUTHOR

SAMUEL MARZIOLI is a Filipino-American author of dark fiction. His work has appeared in numerous publications and podcasts, including *The Best of Apex Magazine*, Flame Tree's *Asian Ghost Short Stories*, *The Dread Machine*, and *LeVar Burton Reads*. He has a chapbook called *Symphony of the Night*, with illustrations by Luke Spooner, and a horror collection called *Hollow Skulls and Other Stories*. You can find more information about his work at marzioli.blogspot. com or follow him on Twitter @marzioli.

LINKS

Author blog: marzioli.blogspot.com
Twitter: @marzioli

This Kind of Darkness

by Kristin Peterson

You might wonder how conjoined twins can experience privacy and lonesome peace from one another. In our case, I used to think it was partly due to the pills Ellie takes for her insomnia. When we were little, she fussed and refused to sleep. Turns out it was because of the incessant shrieks of blood, like a recording from Hell, gushing through Ellie's ears and body, propelled by her gigantic heart, which is continuously growing grotesque offshoots. Arms and fingerlike extensions branching from the mighty organ. The doctors cannot explain why. I personally think her heart is searching for true love, ready to embrace the man who sees her for who she is, who knows who he is, and can see a future for them together. Ellie deserves a lifetime of happy, sunny days. I hoard the darkness for myself.

I would give anything to feel my own heart beating inside my chest, but Ellie has the one we share in hers. She probably yearns for the deep breaths of air I can take, ferocious and fresh as the river galloping and frothing past our house, ripped from existence in ravenous bites I swallow whole. I could ask her, but we haven't spoken to each other since she caught her husband passed out on top of me in bed a few days ago.

Ellie and I are connected above our hips, side by side, through a belt of flesh that could easily be severed to separate us. However, Ellie depends upon my lungs as much as I need her heart. My heart stopped growing in utero. Now it's a calcified vestige I keep locked in my ribcage like a stone baby. My lungs, though, are strong and voluminous enough to keep us both well-oxygenated. Ellie's never developed beyond two hollow primordia.

Our bodies continue to amaze the doctors. *The intricacy of arteries and veins connecting you is a thing of beauty*, they muse. *The adaptive capabilities of the human body are to be marveled. Isn't it all so utterly fascinating?* The right side of Ellie's big, strong heart pushes our stale blood to my lungs for the refreshing capture of oxygen and back to the left side to supply first her body then mine.

Ellie is the smart, pretty, poetic one. I'm the hideous appendage she hauls around, reduced to a portable ventilator every time we leave the house. When we used to go out clubbing with her friends, I was Ellie's interpreter. Because she can't breathe, there's no air to pass through her vocal cords. Instead, she taps Morse code messages onto my fingertips, an excruciatingly slow form of communication everyone else tolerates because of her hypnotic allure. If I change her words, she pinches me. Hard. If I suggest we learn sign language, she pinches me. Inevitably I pinch back. When we were kids, our fights were impossible to break up. Our parents and teachers found it best to let us get all that bad energy out of our systems since they couldn't separate us anyway. Ellie's skin glowing in a shaft of sunlight, beautiful as all get out, mine smudged with grime in a shadow, we would eventually fall asleep exhausted with a flattened palm on the other's cheek.

I believe I tried to absorb Ellie into my own body before we were born. The doctors dismiss me, say that's fantasy. I'd like to devour her now. They consult other doctors around the world. No records from ancient or modern times describe our unique union of bodies. The instances that come closest are the types where the twins are attached at the chest and share two fused hearts. Imagine the claustrophobia of having the front of your body pressed up against another person's your entire life. And them doing something stupid that makes you angry, so you become enraged because looking at their face is like looking in the mirror.

———————————

Night after night lately, we go to bed before Ellie's husband, Todd, arrives home from work. She leaves his dinner in the oven, and we walk upstairs. Ellie takes two sleeping pills—one for each of us. It's difficult to tell when she's asleep since she can't snore or make other sleeping noises with her breath. I rely on her heartbeats to let me know. Still, she meditates, which lowers her pulse rate, so I'm never completely sure.

It is truly a mystery how I've grown to tolerate the pills and Ellie hasn't. I suppose it's because her body soaks it all up before the medication can reach me. It used to put us both to sleep right away. Now it affects her the same as always, but I stay up reading late into the night. When Todd's truck pulls into the driveway, I turn off my lamp, hide the book, and pretend to sleep. Slow, convincing breaths. There's nothing worse than being alone with Todd.

He creaks open the bedroom door, and I hope he lands next to Ellie. Or better, he misses our gigantic bed altogether and passes out on the floor. Tonight, he falls onto Ellie, unbuckles his belt, then snores before releasing a single button on his pants. She remains asleep, so I push him off her. He rolls over onto his back and snores more loudly with his mouth open.

We sleep in a king size bed. Ellie and I are in the middle and Todd's on her side. The idea was I'd have a husband, too.

———————

Before Todd, we'd go out and stay up all night. I'd stand beside Ellie's radiance until I was but a shadow mingling with hers on the floor. Sometimes I'd break into countless dark silhouettes under strobing lights or a disco ball. In situations where someone needs a translator, most people ignore the person they're talking to and focus on the interpreter. In our case, they're drawn to Ellie, her beauty and charm, her kindness and eloquence. I'm kicked to the side, forgotten, drowning in Ellie's goodness. Absorbing more delicious darkness.

Now that Ellie and Todd are settled, married folk, we don't party all that often. Maybe once a month Ellie gets Todd to relent and take us for a night out. Last time she arranged a blind date for me with one of his coworkers. Despite my expectations based upon his taste in friends, the guy wasn't repulsive. Todd's amplified swagger gives away his entire personality, his outside and inside exact replicas of each other. Luckily, most of the time he's out of the house selling new and used cars for his family's dealership and drinking with friends until the bars close. He and I rarely speak to each other. I hardly know him. Ellie says I don't understand the strong, silent type, that he is gentle and kind, that there's a depth to him he shares only with her when I put on my noise canceling headphones so I can listen to music or immerse myself in thought or books to give them some time alone together.

Ellie is tired of me bringing any old guy home, especially the ones I meet on dating apps. Her point is valid. Many of them see us as freaks, some discover fetishes they never knew they had. Todd punches the ones who propose a foursome. When Ellie pulls the curtain down the middle of our bed, it's like a wall of solitude we can throw between our minds. Not that we're telepathic.

•————————————•

What are you thinking about? Ellie's brushing my hair after our afternoon shower. This is the first time she's communicated with me in a week. She taps words on my arm with her free hand.

I turn my head to face her. "Nothing happened between Todd and me."

I know.

"How?"

Let me show you two things. The second will hurt, the worst pain beyond what you can imagine. But it's short lived and replaced with a lasting euphoria. She places the hairbrush on her bedside stand, pulls out two sleeping pills, and downs them. We crawl under the blankets.

She's awake fifteen minutes later, an hour, two hours. *So, you see, you're not the only one who's built a tolerance to them.*

"Why don't you tell the doctor you need a higher dose?"

Because they still take the edge off the noise and because I prefer to be conscious while one or the other of us is about to be ravished without our consent. She does know. Thank goodness he's never succeeded in getting his pants unbuttoned before passing out.

"Are you afraid of him?"

No, but I fear marrying him was a mistake. I'd prefer someone who doesn't have to get obliterated every night to come home to me.

"Have you talked to him about this?" In my opinion, Todd's only redeeming quality is that he remembers Morse code from when he was a Boy Scout. "When you two are together, I do my best to give you privacy by traveling somewhere else in my mind."

That's our next step. You and I are going to visit that other place together, where I go every night, like we used to when we were girls.

I don't speak or blink.

Do you remember?

"No."

That's okay. I'll lead you there and then to others connected to it like the multiple arms of a terrifying but beloved deity.

I think about beeping telegraphs from old movies. The message becomes fainter, unintelligible to my mind, but my body responds like it understands and so does my subconscious, which rises to the surface ready for action. Both are stimulated by the thought of journeying to visit a voracious, multi-armed god. I imagine it with tusks jutting from its lower jaw, walking on legs and arms toward us, ready to consume me, leaving Ellie whole by taking me away. She's the one who deserves to be loved. The liquid void inside me, viscous and black as used motor oil, assures me I don't. I'm especially not worthy of Ellie's love. It'll be enough to be eaten by this divine beast. Perhaps it will restore the balance of our world. Ellie would tell me I'm a narcissist to think this way, that the universe doesn't revolve around me, but I can feel the chaos inside seeping from my pores, drenching everything with my endless supply of discontent and vitriol.

Ellie places my hand on her chest. The rising full moon shines in her big brown eyes that glimmer with delight. I take a breath so deep it submerges us. Her heart pounds, its fists knocking on my fingers and palm. She's giving me a tasting sampler of the heart's many languages. How she discriminates between joyful anticipation and nervousness, I don't know. I feel both now, I think.

The chirping of a million crickets and frogs and buzzing cicadas crowd the night air filled to bursting with humidity. Ellie says not to worry. What we feel is not anxiety but excitement. She closes her eyes and so do I, chasing the ghostly trail of sparks she leaves behind.

It hurts like Ellie said it would, like my being is tearing itself from my body. More pain than I've ever known. The fingerlike offshoots of Ellie's heart release me from inside, but her hand clenches mine to make sure we don't lose each other in the ether.

"This way." Ellie can speak here although she cannot breathe. Her voice is nothing like I imagined. Mine is raspy like the scuttling of mice in the walls, but hers is melodic as a cradlesong.

"Where are we?" I can't see anything in the dark.

"The place where hope resides, where dreams are born, where nightmares visit."

"But it's so bleak. Why would my hopes and dreams be anywhere nearby?"

"Where else but nestled in the deepest despair? Lie down here with me on the lawn." She pulls me to the ground. "Like salmon, they return to their birthplaces after life-long odysseys into the unknown."

This is where my future meets my past, where love and acceptance are inseparable, where maybe for one flash I can truly live in the eternal present.

The grass is soft and dewy, dense, like moss velvet. It's the most comfortable bed I've known. My head is untroubled and pain-free, my muscles relaxed, my body light as dandelion fluff.

"Close your eyes." Ellie lies next to me, farther

away than usual but close enough for us to hold hands. "Don't let go yet."

I breathe the fresh air like I'm drinking from the headwaters of our river's glacier melt.

She squeezes my hand. "Now open them."

"I don't see anything."

"Be patient."

I wait. A bright, unwavering planet appears above, followed by more planets and twinkling stars. Soon the sky is saturated with them, like they form one entity, the singularity smeared across eternity.

"Wish upon a shooting star." Ellie's pointing to a meteor shower. "I choose that one."

She closes her eyes while she makes her wish then pulls me up so we can run hand in hand now that the night sky lights our way. Eventually, we let go of each other.

An orange glow invites us. This beacon is a resting volcano.

Ellie walks to the edge of the crater, where she motions me to follow. "Isn't this the most beautiful thing you've ever seen?"

"Where are we?"

"Inside my thoughts."

"We've never seen a volcano."

"I believe my mind is representing it as my heart."

"Are you sure we're not out in the universe?"

"The universe is inside and outside us. We're seeing ripples of both. The liminal zone where my thoughts lap at the shoreline." She takes my hand again. "Come. I'll show you more."

We run fast as mustangs across a high plains desert, alert for the eternal threats of quicksand and flashfloods rampant in the books Ellie and I loved to read when we were little, until we come to a town. Our town. Sagebrush and cacti give way to a paved grid of roads lined with lush maple and oak trees. A spaghetti western song of screams and harmonicas fades into sixties pop music, a trio of women in beehives, winged eyeliner, and miniskirts singing to us at the city limit. Men in sarapes, cowboy hats, and spurs flee back into the desert.

The women call us Baby. *Baby, Baby. Here come our babies.* They harmonize like angels.

We wave as we pass by, but their song follows us as if we have them in our ears.

Ellie pauses. "Who was that boy who was mean to us in middle school?"

"Can you be more specific?"

"The one who spoke to you but not me."

"Ellie, Derek was always nice to both of us. Other than you, he's the only person our age who's ever paid attention to me."

"Well, I was excluded from your conversations."

"That's not true. You didn't want to read the books we were discussing and refused to suggest any you'd like." I think Derek didn't know how to engage Ellie, although he tried every time he and I spoke.

"Anyway. What was his name?"

"I already told you. Derek. Our mechanic."

"I wasn't aware." Ellie doesn't pay attention when we take our car in for tune-ups and repairs. She's forever angry because I'm on the left, so I get to drive our cool seventies sedan around. We own the old car because it has bench seats and a column shifter. I'm eternally resentful that I have to chauffeur her everywhere.

When Ellie gets bossy while we're driving, I take turns fast and unpredictably. We slide on the vinyl seats in our dresses. In the summer we stick to them when we wear shorts, ripping our bare thighs as we screech around corners. Ellie never learns. She keeps scrolling through an endless stream of TikTok videos punctuated with breaks for posting selfies and tapping hearts on Instagram, only addressing me to complain about my driving or to convince me we need a ton of indoor plants like literally everyone else our age. She dismisses me when I remind her how we don't have enough light in our home. This hunger for plants is leading to the extinction of peat moss habitats.

She grows bored, wanting to explore this place. "Let's find Derwood's house."

"Who?"

"You know, Darren, our mechanic."

"Derek. He lives next to his shop."

"Where's that?"

Even in wherever we are—the universe inside her thoughts—it's my job to take Ellie around. "This way."

"Where do you think his bedroom is?" She's heading toward the right.

"How would I know? Let's split up." What a glorious thing to be able to do something alone. "You take the front, and I'll go around back. Do you still hear that music?"

"Yes, it's the theme song for our town. Let's do this."

Ellie finds Derek's room immediately and explains it away. "The houses in this neighborhood all have the same floorplan." She avoids looking into my eyes.

We peek inside the window. Derek is splayed across his bed as if he were on the rack.

"Time for some harmless torture." She rubs her hands together.

"Like I said, Derek's always been kind. And he gives us huge discounts."

"Ah, a romantic wooing you with half price spark plugs."

"Discounted labor, not parts."

"Whatever. We don't have all night."

Ellie enters through the open window. It's barely cracked, but she oozes through like a snake slithering out of its old skin and pulls me in after her. My bones loosen and come undone. The sight of my body bending in unnatural ways nauseates me. I vomit on Derek's floor.

"Sorry."

"For what?" Ellie's circling his bed.

"The noise. Did I wake him?"

"He can't hear us when he's asleep. Here's the deal. We're nightmares, which means we sit on his chest so he can't breathe, and he's paralyzed."

"What do we get out of it?"

"Fun."

"But I like him. Remember last time we took the car in he invited us to pick peaches from the tree in the backyard?"

"Suit yourself." She jumps onto Derek's chest where she sits smiling and reading a book of poetry she took from a stack on his bedstand.

"I find it upsetting the glee you're getting from cutting off his air supply when I'm the one with our lungs. It's like you want to kill me."

"Ooh. Look how he's freezing up. He's aware but can't move and can't scream for help. Poor Derwood." She caresses his face then dismounts. "Your turn."

Derek gasps for air. I wait until he makes eye contact with me, then pull myself onto his chest. His face darkens, his eyes bulge. I'm unable to continue. Ellie's own eyes are wild, their whites gleaming in the starlight. I slide to lie beside Derek, combing his curly hair with my fingers while he catches his breath.

You've finally returned to me. Derek kisses me. *I love you, Ellie.*

Even in this nowhere place everyone loves Ellie.

I'm about to return to his chest but Derek squints, regards me for a moment.

Wait. You're the other one.

The chest it is. Although I'm determined to crush him, he pulls me in for a longer kiss on the lips and a constellation around my face.

He stops. *I've always liked you best.*

"Let's go, *now*." Ellie's furious. She pulls me away from Derek, through the window, and into the night. "I don't know all the rules of this place, but the last thing we need is for you to have a spectral baby."

"That seems unlikely."

"We'll be at peak fertility in three hours. It would be unseemly if you got pregnant before I did."

"From his otherworldly sperm? Little phantoms propelled by their rotating celestial tails?"

"Stop it. We need to get home before Todd. He and I are trying for a baby."

"What? We need to kick him to the curb. Isn't that what all this is about? Escape."

"It's *an* escape. I love him with my entire heart."

I have little patience for Ellie when she defends Todd. "He doesn't deserve you. Besides, how did you decide to have a baby without involving me in the conversation?"

"Love letters, texts, emails. I *am* literate."

"I mean, how could you make such a huge decision without discussing it with me? And a team of doctors? It could be dangerous for us."

"I'm willing to take that chance. You and I have always dreamt of having children."

"True. But those were youthful fantasies. We didn't understand their implications."

"Don't worry. You'll make a great aunt."

"That's not what I'm worried about."

"We have to hurry. Todd's home." She takes my hand in hers.

I blink, and we're back in our corporeal bodies. Todd's unlocking the front door. It's early in the evening.

Ellie taps her fingertips on mine. *Let's put the finishing touches on dinner.* When we sit up, she's arranging her hair and pinching her cheeks for color.

I relent and we hurry sideways down the staircase to greet Todd. We're doing crab walks today. Tomorrow is Egyptians. The day after is the Norma Desmond walk.

Ellie speaks through me. "Darling, welcome home. I missed you terribly." She rushes to Todd, dragging me along like a ragdoll. "We've made you a lovely, *light* dinner." She winks at him although he hasn't looked at her yet.

"Bring me a beer, babe." He swats her behind, leans back in his recliner, and turns on the TV with the remote. The man is already acting like a father—a natural.

"But sweetie, tonight's the night."

"You got that right, babe. Monday night football."

He is focused on a television commercial, still avoiding the sight of us.

"Honey. Remember what we talked about. Optimal fecundity happening now."

"Oh. That." He sighs and looks at the pregame show on the TV, then the wall clock and Ellie, pauses a moment, and grabs her hand. "I'll watch the game while we eat."

We fly up the stairs, land on the bed, and Ellie pulls the curtain between us before they begin. Todd has four minutes until kickoff. He needs two with Ellie before he's back downstairs popping open a beer can and belching loudly.

I'm worried because Ellie's not moving. "Are you okay?"

Yeah, I'm supposed to lie on my back with my legs elevated for a few minutes.

"Another thing you could've told me."

You're right. I'm sorry for excluding you.

"It's okay. I want us to be happy."

———

That night Ellie doesn't take her sleeping pills but instead waits for Todd. When he ascends the steps, I put away my book and turn off the light. Ellie smooths her lingerie and whips the curtain between us.

Todd's clothes hit the floor, and the bed groans from his weight. "You want me again, don't you, babe?"

I close my eyes and try to remember what it felt like to follow Ellie to that place. She said it was a voyage into her mind. I'll sail off into my own. Instead, I wake the next morning, sunlight dappling Ellie's smiling face as she sleeps. Todd's gone to work.

Ellie opens her eyes and yawns.

I seize her hand. "Teach me how to get to that other place again. I'll try for Derek's ghost baby so we can go through this experience together. I hate being left out of everything."

She guides me back. It's daytime, bandidos tearing after us through desert scrub. One succumbs to quicksand, camouflaged and deadly as black ice. His horse screams, white eyes rolling in their sockets, the lather on its neck visible. It pulls itself out, occasional bubbles from the sunken rider breaking the surface. Ellie and I gallop ahead on horseback as the outlaws try to save their fallen comrade.

At the city limits, where it is nighttime, the trio of pop singers welcomes us. *Baby, Baby.* The center woman is holding a baby. *Come to me, Baby.*

Ellie dismounts and takes the tiny, swaddled cherub. "Just look at her. So precious." She gazes up at me. "You go to Derek. I'll catch up."

My horse and I prance into town toward Derek's house.

Derek awakes with me on his chest. I slip down to sit on the bed so he can breathe. Here in this place tonight, I wear too much black eyeliner, cherry lipstick, and a sleeveless rubber catsuit. I'm covered with tattoos and piercings and smoke Indonesian clove cigarettes.

Derek takes a drag, tells me how often he's fantasized about me. I kiss his silken lips, run my hands down to his and examine his calloused fingers with my own. He kicks off the blankets, lays me down, and climbs on top of me.

How do I remove this thing? He's reaching around feeling for a zipper or some other way into the suit.

"No idea."

We kiss as he feels between my legs.

I found the entrance. He has that dopey guy look on his face, his eyes half closed, then squeezed shut as he thrusts. With each moan, each movement, he tears at the catsuit that now hangs off me in strips. He sucks my nipples and glides his tongue down to my clitoris, pleasuring me until I climax. While I'm still pulsating, wrapped in the luxury of desire, I pull him inside me. Without a single movement from him, I bring him to orgasm with the uncontrolled, throbbing aftermath of my own. He kisses me before collapsing onto the bed. I lie on my back with my knees on my chest like Ellie did.

She's at the window, nursing her baby. "A few more minutes and we should go." She smiles wider than I've ever seen. Rivulets of tears meander through the valleys surrounding her cheeks as she sways and sings lullabies.

———————•———————

Nine months later Ellie and I are in labor. Midwives and birthing centers couldn't take us because of our high-risk factors, so we long ago resigned ourselves to giving birth in the hospital. On a bariatric bed instead of in a pool. Each of us has a doula to support us. We hired lawyers to draw up paperwork for all possibilities—if one or the other dies, if both die, if it's a choice between mother and baby. Grim stuff. Todd moved in with his parents a few months back. Derek has no idea he's about to be a father. I don't know if our child will be human. Ellie's ecstatic.

Alarms blast from the machines we're hooked up to. Doctors and nurses rally. After efforts to stabilize us fail, they mobilize to rush us to the operating room for emergency C-sections. Ellie and I hold hands as we careen toward the unknown. We're cold. She smiles while I breathe deeply to calm us. The doulas are arguing as they run behind. I instructed mine to advocate for Ellie in this situation. She told hers to do the same for me.

Ellie takes me to the other place where we picnic under a lone palo verde tree. We're in our favorite dresses. She tells me she loves me more than she could love anyone, save for our wee ones who are anxious to see the world. Cousins who will grow up like sisters.

The outlaws watch us from the plateau above. Their theme song haunts us. We wave from our gingham blanket, invite them to sit. They remind us to beware of flash floods and quicksand before bolting away in the opposite direction. Laughing, I look over at Ellie in time to see the tips of her long hair—the last of her to be swallowed whole by the desert floor. Reaching to pull her out, I thrash my arms in the quicksand but can't find her. I've gotten as far as I can without being pulled in myself.

Crying and desperate, I lie next to the spot where Ellie disappeared, so tired. Nothing of her remains, like she never existed. I'd follow her, but the ground is solid now. This is what it's like to be alone, what I wished for every time Ellie and I blew out our birthday candles. Well, when I blew them out. I want to know her wishes.

The cycle of days and nights here mimic those on Earth, but at accelerated, inconsistent rates. I never wander far from the tree, hoping the earth will spit Ellie back out to me. After what seems like an eternity since losing her, I realize I have no need for food, water, or sleep. I keep watch always.

The outlaws warn me. *A rider approaches.*

I stand, unaware of how long I've been sitting against the tree. A long trail of dust crescendos into the sky, the rider heading straight for me. I feel Ellie again, as if she were still a part of me. That's love, I think. When two become one, when you need the other to survive, when you are better together than apart.

"Whoa." Ellie slows her appaloosa to a stop. Her face is aglow with joy as she slides down and runs to me for a hug. She's wearing a backpack.

"I've missed you." Tears of relief, of bottled worry, of lonesome heartbreak stream down my face.

"Look who I've brought for a visit." She carefully removes the backpack, which is a doublewide carrier for infants.

Two perfect, beautiful babies coo and wiggle on the picnic blanket, tight fists holding the other's hand.

"Meet your daughter. I named her after you." She passes a baby to me.

"Hello, little one." I kiss her all over. She emanates a fresh scent like someone who's just come in from the cold.

Ellie's sitting on the blanket, nursing her baby. "It's time for their feeding."

My baby cries in frustration as she searches for a nipple with her face like a blind, newborn kitten. Soon she's wailing. My breasts grow heavy in response. I unbutton the front of my dress, fast as I can. After a few tries, I get her to latch on.

I feel complete, in the moment. Ellie lets me enjoy this gift, not mentioning what I already know. The tiny miracle in my arms falls asleep after depleting my milk supply. I had no idea the sound of a healthy baby could be so comforting. It's their breath when they pause to inhale and exhale through their noses while nursing. A gentle rhythm.

"Thank you for this, Ellie."

"I need to tell you something."

"Please don't say it."

For the first time, Ellie is breathing. She pulls open the top of her dress to show me her sutured incision. "You'll always be with me." She rubs her chest, takes a deep breath.

I'm disintegrating, no more than a desert mirage. Ellie rushes to hold me. She sidles up on my right, where she's lived our entire existence. I close my eyes to warm, black velvet and rest my head on her chest, listening to her heart and my lungs, like holding a conch to my ear and hearing the ocean. This is what I've given everything for, this kind of darkness.

Author's Note on "This Kind of Darkness"

Recently, I have been writing clusters of stories centered around different themes—in this case duality. I created a situation in which my conjoined twins could not be separated in order to explore how we all can distort the way we perceive ourselves and others. Despite being genetically identical and living in the same environment their entire lives, the sister with the lungs believes she is unattractive and unworthy of the love that her beautiful, charismatic twin should receive. She worships her sister, who carries their heart, but also resents her many flaws. Although the two are individuals, they jointly form a metaphorical whole. Together and independently, they are complex people who form complex relationships with each other and their world.

About the Author

Originally from the Cascade mountains of far-northern California, KRISTIN PETERSON lives in the Caribbean with her family and familiars. Her work has appeared or is forthcoming in *Thinking Horror: A Journal of Horror Philosophy*, *Vastarien: A Literary Journal*, and *Never Wake: An Anthology of Dream Horror*, among others.

Links

Facebook: www.facebook.com/kristin.peterson.121
Instagram: www.instagram.com/krpeterson77/
Twitter: twitter.com/krpeterson77

Acknowledgments

Thanks to all the authors whose work helped bring this collection together. Many thanks to those who helped along the way, namely Richard Thomas and Suzi Madron. Endless thanks to cover artist, Greg Chapman, and book designer/artist/author/creative renaissance man, Todd Keisling, for the wonderful design of this little ol' book.

D. Alexander Ward
Gina Scapellato

www.ingramcontent.com/pod-product-compliance
Lightning Source LLC
Chambersburg PA
CBHW031132130726
47988CB00006B/2338